One Two
Buckle My Shoe

E J LAMPREY

DEDICATED TO V.E.L.

who always believed in me,

and who loved whodunits

CONTENTS

A note to the reader

No book set in Scotland could be without occasional moments of Scottish. Beyond the soft burr of the accents, which will have to wait for the audio version, it is very nearly a language on its own, descriptive and pungent. Some words shared with English are pronounced differently, and some words are unique to the country. In Scotland, you would chap on a poorly neighbour's door and offer to get their messages (knock and offer to do their shopping). All Scots speak English, but few can resist the temptation to slide sideways into the joy of Scots every now and then and my characters are no different.

*The general meaning should always be clear from the context—a brief glossary has been added at the end for easy reference. Definitely is pronounced deffi-NATE-ly in Scotland and has deliberately been spelled **'definately'** in appropriate dialogue. The same applies to other spelling 'errors' spotted in dialogue (jag for injection, drap for drop, deid for dead, etc.). I have kept this to a minimum, to avoid puzzling non-Scottish readers, but hope you will enjoy the occasional reminder that you are north of the border.*

The police force in Scotland changed completely when it became Police Scotland in April 2013. Even before then, the smaller autonomous divisions were being amalgamated. In this one respect, my first two books ignore the march of progress in the fictional town of Onderness

This book is the first in a series, so anyone who read one of the others first and is now backtracking may be surprised that William and Donald only appear for the first time towards the end; even Vivian doesn't appear immediately. They are full members of the quartet in the other books.

By the same author

Three Four Knock On My Door

Five Six Pick Up Sticks

Seven Eight Play It Straight

THE PURPLE HAT

There's an old story about the ages of women, which goes something like this:

Age 5: She looks in the mirror and sees a princess.

Age 15: She looks at herself and sees an Ugly Sister (Mom, I can't go to school looking like this!)

Age 25: She looks at herself and agonizes 'too fat/too thin, too short/too tall, too straight/too curly'

Age 40: She looks at herself and sees 'too fat/too thin, too short/too tall, too straight/too curly' but tells herself at least she looks tidy.

Age 50: She looks at herself and sees lines and the first grey hairs, but also wisdom, laughter and ability.

After 60: Doesn't bother to look. Just puts on a purple hat and goes out to have fun with the world.

CHAPTER ONE

It can be hard to pin down exactly when a story starts.
You join this one on the second Thursday in December,
not twenty miles north of Edinburgh …

The caller was very deaf – after twice exhorting the duty
officer to speak up, she gave up and merely repeated
herself.

'This is Elizabeth Campbell, from number one at
Grasshopper Lawns. There's been a murder done. My
dear woman, I can't hear you. Just send a polisman and
I'll tell him all about it.' She hung up with a decisive
click.

'If this is that DJ doing a wind-up call I'll have him on

a charge, so I will,' the duty officer muttered under her breath, but logged the call and passed it on, adding that it wasn't a cry for help, the caller had sounded more annoyed than alarmed.

For that matter it wasn't the first call from the retirement village, although the usual cry was of missing treasures, which turned out not to be missing at all, only misplaced. Any real cause for alarm would be phoned in by one of the Trust's staff, so it was close on an hour before Detective Inspector McLuskie and Sergeant Cameron from the small local division, who had just ended their surveillance of a store owner suspected of selling alcohol to minors, were free to call on the old lady.

Iain McLuskie, new to the Onderness posting, asked the controller to repeat the address and still didn't look confident, but Kirsty Cameron touched his arm reassuringly.

'I ken where it is, Iain, got an aunt living there. Just head towards Linlithgow and turn left after the motorway.'

'Oh aye, that's what she said.' McLuskie put the car into gear. 'You're telling me they're living on that campsite, then.'

Kirsty giggled. 'Grasshopper Lawns is opposite. In fact the campsite is for their visitors, but opens to the public as well.'

'I didn't know there was another retirement place in these parts—that big place near Linlithgow, aye, but nothing local. Keep themselves to themselves, do they?'

'The purple hatters;' Kirsty shot him a mischievous glance, 'started as a joke, but they like it, you *must* have seen them on Thursdays in Onderness, that's the day they come through here to shop and go to the library.'

McLuskie started to laugh. 'I have, then. One old fellow in a purple balaclava, just the other day. He was walking along the road with another old 'un in a purple tweed cap, and a woman in a kind of purple and red turban. Very good!'

~~~

Grasshopper Lawns certainly didn't flaunt its status. The rural road off the A904 was flanked on either side by sturdy stone-built farm walls. On the Grasshopper Lawns side there was a further screening of wintery ornamental hedge with a few rebel twigs poking above its well-pruned even six feet. The first break in the wall had a closed five-bar gate, with a small notice directing callers further down the road to the main house, but when McLuskie did pull into the main entrance and draw up with a brisk scattering of gravel he was impressed.

The building before them was built on classic lines, either of stone or stone-faced, and perfectly proportioned to its three levels, well furnished with windows, and fronted with a flourish of stone steps. In view of its purpose, curving sturdy hand-rails flanked the stairs and a discreet ramp inclined gently to one side. To either side of the parking area at the front of the house, a paved and well-maintained service road was tucked away against the original farm walls. On the inner side of the service road there were long low blocks of bungalow units surrounding a park-like attractive garden of generous proportions, to judge by the glimpse through the gap between the house and the first block.

The two police officers strode into the large entrance hall, greeted with raised brows by Megan, the front-of-house receptionist, and watched with interest by three older people reading newspapers in the sofas set about the big area, and two fairly elderly Labradors in large dog beds. Megan, an attractively rounded woman in her forties, greeted Kirsty by name with a smile, then turned her attention fully back to McLuskie, who explained that they wanted to see Mrs Campbell.

'Miss Campbell.' Megan corrected gently. 'But I didn't know Betsy needed the police? If you'll wait just a moment I'll give her a ring.' Her brows drew together as she held the house-phone to her ear. 'She's not answering …'

'The controller did say she was very deaf.' Iain McLuskie offered, and Megan nodded at him.

'She is, but her phone has a flashing light system all round her apartment. Oh dear—Jamie, do you think—'

'Oh aye, I'll tek the polis to her.' Jamie relinquished his newspaper with alacrity and heaved himself to his feet with the aid of a particularly fine silver-ornamented mahogany walking stick. The December day was mild, and he contented himself with facing the elements in a tweed cap and a well-worn tweed jacket, leaving a scarf and greatcoat still draped over the back of the sofa. He led the way briskly down the ramp and plunged through a gap in the winter-thin rhododendrons onto a covered walkway.

'You'll be a regular visitor then, missus?' he asked Kirsty, who explained about her aunt.

'Oh aye,' Jamie chuckled. 'Edge is a card, she is. Actually, you look like her, now's I'm looking. It's right here.'

The door of number one was shut, but Jamie played a jaunty flourish on the bell, then cracked the door ajar, peered inside, and pushed it open. They followed him into a spotlessly tidy kitchen, leading to a short passageway. Doors opened either side to a bathroom and walk-in closet, and the door ahead stood half open. He knocked again, peered round the door, nodded over his shoulder to the police and mouthed *'sleeping'* before turning back to roar in a voice unsuspected in one of his slender frame, 'Betsy, hen, here's the polis to see you.'

McLuskie, looking past him, saw a large woman in a comfortable armchair, her head to one side and her mouth open as she slept on. Or not—gently putting Jamie to one side he entered the room and hunkered down next to the woman, touching her arm. 'Miz Campbell?' He moved his hand to lay the length of his palm on her arm, then turned his head to Kirsty. 'Can you get Jamie out of here?' he asked quietly, but Jamie was having none of it.

'Is she deid?' he demanded and when McLuskie lifted his shoulders in a faint shrug that was nonetheless confirmation, his well-worn face creased further. 'Ach, no. She made grand scones, so she did.'

~~~

'Normally we wouldn't assume the worst.' McLuskie told the administrator, who nodded in understanding.

'Oh, I do agree. She phoned you, she said she had a murder to report, and she herself was dead when you arrived. I completely understand, of course. I only hope it doesn't get into the papers, that sort of thing is so bad for a place like this.'

'An investigative team had to be called in, under the circumstances, but until we get the report back on how she died, we're not necessarily treating it as suspicious. But in view of what she told the controller, we would like to know who else has died lately?' McLuskie persisted and the administrator narrowed her eyes in thought, then pressed a button on her intercom.

'Megan, dear, can you find me the termination files for the—I think for the last year should do it?'

'Are there so many deaths?' Kirsty was horrified but Harriet Blake smiled reassuringly. She was a heavily-built woman, unflatteringly dressed in a severe pin-striped jacket and skirt, and her face, in repose, looked stern. Her smile, however, was particularly charming and more in keeping with the soft silk tie of her spotless white blouse.

'Oh no, my dear, but I don't like to rely on my memory—I'm nearly retirement age myself, you know, I find it best to work with records. I can think of two, only one of them recent, but poor Betsy could be meaning someone further back. Thank you Megan;' as the other entered with a slim sheaf of three files and put them on the desk. 'Three? Oh, that'll be Angus, of course.'

'Maybe you could join us?' McLuskie looked up at Megan.

'I've left Josie on the desk.' She glanced at Harriet uncertainly.

'Josie gets a bit fidgety.' Harriet explained, a bit apologetically. 'She's absolutely fine to cover Megan for a few minutes at a time but we'd normally get one of the others for Megan's lunch break, for instance.'

McLuskie conceded that Josie's relief outweighed Megan's participation and she left the room. He looked at Harriet with his brows up. 'Any volunteers you can get, eh?'

'Oh, not at all.' She separated the three files on her desk. 'Several of the residents take it in turns to work a standby shift, they get house credits for it which can be very useful.'

She shot him a quick glance under her rather heavy brows. 'House credits can be spent on drinks at our little pub, or meals here, you know. Some residents are on quite tight budgets, so it frees up cash. Some of them work part-time in the kitchen, or helping out generally. We couldn't run this place to the standard we do without them, either—it all works out very well. Josie's delightful, and very popular with callers, but she's easily distracted. If there isn't much going on she gets bored and if too much happens at once she gets flustered. We work to people's strengths, but also to their limitations. Now, the most recent first. Moses McKenzie died only a week ago. It was very sad, he choked to death in his apartment, and although there are panic buttons all over the place he never reached one, so nobody went to his aid. I don't think that can be what Betsy meant, because choking—well, you can't murder someone that way, can you? Nobody could force someone to choke.' She selected the death certificate from the papers in the file and passed it over for inspection.

'Then there's Betty Taylor, Elizabeth Taylor she liked to be called, but most people called her Betty. She died in August of pneumonia, but she was in the hospital in Larbert by then. We have a Frail Care centre here in the house, with a fine matron, but you can't take chances with pneumonia, you know. They call it the old man's friend, but Betty wasn't old. Not yet seventy. It was very sad but again, I can't see it could have been murder?' Another death certificate passed across the desk, exchanged for the first, which was carefully re-filed.

'And Angus Burns;' she flicked swiftly through the bottom file, her heavy brows drawing together. 'Oh dear. There was an inquest for Angus, because he took an overdose of his sleeping pills, and his friends insisted it couldn't have been deliberate. The procurator fiscal eventually signed it off as misadventure rather than suicide. Betsy could have meant Angus although she

8

never met him, she moved here after he died.' This time the returning death certificate was exchanged for the procurator fiscal's report, which McLuskie flipped through before handing it to Kirsty.

'What did you think at the time?' he asked Harriet, who lifted her heavy shoulders very slightly.

'I don't have as much to do with the residents as Megan, she's the best person to ask. I did know Angus, because he was a rip-roaring old character, hugely popular, had some wonderful stories, but he was getting a little doddery, well over eighty. The life he'd had, so full of adventure, going on safari in Africa and sailing to Australia—I did think he had wanted to escape the indignities of extreme old age, so I assumed it was suicide. But as I say, I didn't know him as well as his friends did, and they were very convincing at the inquest. Back in the day being a suicide would have meant he couldn't be buried in a churchyard. That doesn't matter nowadays, but the stigma of suicide still matters to some. I was glad when the coroner came up with a misadventure verdict.'

'And Miz Campbell—how was her health? If she hadn't phoned us, would you have called us when she was found?'

'Yes I would.' Harriet Blake said decisively. 'Betsy Campbell was, apart from her increasing deafness, a hale and hearty woman in her early sixties, one of our best bakers, and as fit as a flea. She not only joined the aerobics class here every day, she was a great walker and hasn't had so much as a sniffle all winter. I am extremely surprised, and disturbed, to hear of her death.'

'One last question,' Kirsty leant forward. 'If you'll permit—you said you were near retirement age yourself. Would you want to live here?'

'I already do.' Harriet smiled thinly. 'The Administrator position includes an apartment on the third floor of this house, but I know what you mean, would I want to stay on as a resident when I retire. I certainly would if I could. However, it isn't cut-and-dried, there's a waiting list of nearly a hundred approved applicants.'

She glanced from one to the other. 'Grasshopper Lawns was founded, and is still largely funded, by a Trust set up by a very wealthy businesswoman who, as she approached retirement age, was determined to spend her leisured years in the company of interesting people. The place is unique, and we get hundreds of applications every year. To be approved, you have to be without family,' she bent her index finger down, 'you have to have led an unusual life, or had unusual experiences,' second finger down, 'and you have to be in good health, mobile and independent. Many applicants are only in their fifties. Then you get interviewed by at least three members of the admissions board, and if they rubber-stamp your application you get added to the approved list. She was still here when I became Administrator about eight years ago, and she insisted the admissions board included not only the Trust staff but five representatives from the residents. Every application has to be signed off by at three people, at least one of whom has to be a resident. Four years after coming here I applied for an eventual place and I am an approved applicant, but not even close to the top of the list. So, yes, I would become a resident if I could, but I may end up having to go elsewhere.'

~~~

'She was fibbing a bit there.' Kirsty said quietly to McLuskie as they made their way back to the ground floor to see Megan, and he shot her a quick sidelong look.

'Aye, I thought so too, couldn't put my finger on it but if she knows, or suspects, someone is knocking residents off, I reckon she'd not be so keen to live here, eh?' He gave a short laugh. 'What do you reckon her unusual experiences were? She's a dead ringer for my English teacher at school, couldn't be more conventional. Bet your aunt isn't.'

'Oh aye.' Kirsty grinned reminiscently. 'Aunt Edge is a corker. Lived all over the world, widowed twice and left comfortably off each time, but also made a packet writing TV dramas until she retired, she's not one who has to work for house credits, she's absolutely rolling. And a wicked sense of humour, too. She's top, my aunt.'

'I was thinking,' McLuskie glanced across, 'we don't know yet if it's a case. But if it is, mebbe your aunt could give us a bit of background on the place? Or were you planning to play the whole thing down so as not to alarm her?'

'Alarm Aunt Edge!' Kirsty gave an involuntary hoot of laughter. 'She'd absolutely love it. She's in number twelve, we can stop by after we've talked to Megan. If she's home, of course, her social life is ten times more hectic than mine.'

~~~

Megan called the distractible Josie to take her place on the desk and, after a quick glance through the door to check the room was empty, led them into a well-stocked library. Comfortable seats were placed at convenient intervals and she pulled one over towards two others and gestured to them to sit down.

'Poor Betsy,' she said conventionally. 'I've made Jamie go up to Frail Care to see Matron, he was quite pale. This isn't like an old-age home, you know, where people die all the time, especially when it's somebody quite young and active. It will have been a nasty wee shock for him.'

'We'll mebbe have more questions about Betsy once we get back the results of the autopsy but in fact we wanted to ask a few general questions. You were surprised when we arrived?'

'Well, I was.' Megan nodded vigorously. 'The residents don't normally phone the police direct, because so often they've just got muddled about things, or lost something and think it's been stolen, so they're supposed to report anything odd to me and then I would call if it seemed necessary. What was it Betsy rang about?'

'She had—concerns.' McLuskie said guardedly. 'Missus Blake said you knew the residents probably better than anyone.'

'Me or Matron, yes. I see them every day, and it's part of my job to chat with them, I also organize the house credits rota—did Harriet mention that? Oh right, so you know that some of the residents like to work part-time. Not only for the credits, either, they just like keeping their hand in, so to speak. Betsy was a wonderful baker. And then Matron makes a point of seeing everyone on a regular basis. Some people she sees every day to give out medication. She runs a daily exercise clinic and it's a condition of residence that people go along at least once a week, one way or another she sees everyone at least three times a week to check everyone's chipper, that sort of thing. We had a bit of a tragedy in March, you know, with one of our old guys mismanaging his own medication, so now everything's delivered to the admin office, and Matron makes sure everyone gets their correct daily doses.'

'That would be Angus Burns, then?' McLuskie seized the cue. 'The sleeping pill overdose. So you agree it wasn't suicide?'

'Well, they ruled it wasn't, didn't they? So sad, though. Angus was a regular character, even in a place like this where everyone's got interesting stories to tell, he had a proper fund of them. And he told them well, you couldn't help but laugh. Mentally as sharp as a tack, he spent most of his time on his computer and I know for a fact he had a huge Twitter following—well, I followed him myself. He was hilarious. He had Parkinson's which affected his legs particularly badly, was finding it harder and harder to get about—he'd told me once he'd rather die than leave here, but we're not set up for full invalid care, he would have had to go to a proper facility once he was bedridden. I assumed at the time that his legs had been particularly bad one night and he'd decided the time had come, but there was no note. There was an inquest, and they ruled he'd got confused and taken too many pills, and ever since then Matron controls all medication. It upset everybody.'

'If you don't mind me saying so, you seem more upset about Angus than Betsy?' Kirsty asked shrewdly and Megan blushed.

'Oh—you know—you have your favourites. Betsy and I had our clashes, to be honest, she wasn't always the easiest.' Megan paused for a moment and then went on, picking her words with, both police felt, some care. 'Betsy hadn't been long retired and was used to being in charge of things. She did rub people up the wrong way a bit, and then I'd have to make peace. And someone's sure to tell you she went to Harriet more than once over my head when she felt I wasn't doing my job right. The thing is, a lot of people take time to settle in and she *was* settling. She would have been fine. I can't say we were friendly or even that I liked her but in time she would have made friends and eased up a bit, and I'm sorry she didn't get the chance.'

~~~

'This,' said Kirsty, with the air of one bestowing a treat, 'is my aunt Beulah Edgington Cameron, but she hates being called Beulah. And Aunt Edge, this is Detective Inspector Iain McLuskie, he's worried that you'll go all shaky on us when you hear why we're here. I'm ready to bet that you know already.'

'Of course I do, darling. Jamie rang from Sick Bay to tell me, but Josie had already told Vivian, who had spotted the ambulance, and Vivian told me. Keeping a secret in this place is very nearly impossible. It's very nice to meet you, Iain, and kind of you to be concerned, but you won't need your smelling salts with me or anyone else. She was very much disliked, you know.'

McLuskie blinked at Kirsty's forthright aunt as she waved them into chairs, still talking. Far from being an elderly stooped version of his colleague, she was slim, mischievous, probably only in her late fifties, and unexpectedly attractive. 'They'll never come out and say that, at the house, so I'm telling you. She was very domineering, a great one for organizing and trying to get everyone together to do things. Well, you know, the reason most of us like it here is that nobody does try to force us to be sociable. We're a fiercely independent bunch of individuals who like our own company, like living alone, and like the fact that although we've got all the conveniences of living in an age-friendly environment, we can shut our doors and tell the world to go to hell if we want to. So when you get some hectoring woman on your doorstep three times a week telling you to join a chess club or knit for seafarers or some other pet scheme of hers, and who's too deaf to hear you telling her to go to blazes, well, she got on people's nerves. And she pried, oh my. Her idea of conversation was a stream of questions, she was perfectly exhausting. Always poking around in other people's business. The only nice thing I can say about her was that she was a wonderful baker, her scones were so light you had to hold them down to take a bite out of them, but I'll never know how she got approved by the Board.'

'Is it so difficult?' McLuskie was fascinated and shot a glance at Kirsty who was beaming fondly at her aunt. There was a remarkable family resemblance. Kirsty had flaming exuberant red hair scraped sternly back and her aunt's, not as bright or abundant, was expensively streaked and caught up in a casual and flattering topknot, but their features were virtually identical. And their blunt conversational style—

'Oh my dear, not difficult as such, but; well, I know you met Jamie. Jamie was a mercenary, he's fought in nearly every major or minor war in the last forty years, sometimes he'd fight to put someone in power in a country and two years later he'd be fighting to bring them down again. But he wasn't just a gun for hire, he saved a lot of children who were in very traumatic circumstances and I happen to know several of them chip in towards his keep here, and they write to him from all over the world. He's a lovely chap, Jamie. And maybe you saw Josie, I know it's her day for standby? So demure butter wouldn't melt in her mouth but she used to be a madam, you know. She's very proud of it. Not that it was on her application, she'd also been an actress, but someone apparently found out a couple of years ago and she made no attempt to hide it, she went public and told everyone. She's a perfect example of that old saying that a bad reputation lends lustre to old age. My neighbour is a Russian ballerina who defected before you two were even born—everyone here has a story, which is a good thing because when you get older you tend to think yourself fairly remarkable. Being among other remarkable people keeps it in perspective, stops you being boring. We're all rolling stones in our own way, most of us aren't even Scottish except by choice, we're a very mixed bunch and rather proud of it. And then there's Betsy, and I never did find what was remotely remarkable about her.'

'It isn't a reason to be murdered, Aunt.' Kirsty kept her face straight with some difficulty, and Edge shot her a reproving look.

'I was just saying I didn't know how she got admitted here. Being a prison warder is an unusual job, but not necessarily an interesting one. If I had still been on the admissions board I'd have known at once it was a job that could only attract very bossy, domineering women, which is not at all a Grasshopper trait. She would never talk about it, either, said it would be a violation of their privacy to talk about people she'd known in stir. She didn't seem to see all that poking and prying she did was a violation of *our* privacy, and you know, in a place like this with people like us, there are a lot of secrets. It was only a matter of time before she was murdered. If, of course, she was. Now, it's teatime and Kirsty will tell you there's no point hoping to get a nice cup of tea from me because I can burn water. I want to get up to the house to get all the gossip, you're both welcome to come as my guests and have one of the last Betsy scones. They may be some kind of evidence?'

McLuskie looked at his watch and Kirsty said diffidently, 'It would be a chance to meet more of the suspects?'

He laughed aloud. 'We don't even know if it's a case yet! I want to get back, file today's reports and get a few questions underway, but if you want to stay and—er—interview suspects I can swing by and collect you in an hour?'

She accepted gratefully and he waved cheerfully as he plunged back along the covered walkway towards the car park. Edge, coming up behind her with her handbag over her arm and the apartment keys in her hand, said inquisitively, 'He seems a very nice man?'

'He is.' Kirsty smiled at her aunt. 'And happily married to a very nice woman. He's only been here a month, but I like working with him—and I think he's a good copper. Knows how to ask questions without putting people's backs up. Tell me, Aunt, if Betsy was murdered, who would benefit? Do you have to be rich to live here?'

'Not really.' Edge tucked her hand into her niece's arm as they in turn made their way rather more sedately along the non-slip walkway. 'Because it's run by a Trust, money doesn't really matter. The rents are matched to the state pension. You need either a private pension, or family chipping in, for luxuries, but it isn't money that gets you in the door. As for Betsy, I know she had a very good pension and had sold her flat at a good price because she insisted on telling me, but I haven't a clue who inherits. She'd never married, and she had no family that I knew of, she used to tell me how lucky I was to have you right here in the area. And that was an example of her prying, because you may be sure I never told her I had a niece in the first place. You're my little secret.'

She squeezed Kirsty's arm affectionately as they tackled the side stairs and paused for a moment at the top to catch her breath. 'Right! Teatime!'

The big reception area was now crowded with people all talking at the same time, and the big table that had previously been strewn with newspapers had been laid for afternoon tea, with a chocolate cake taking pride of place and flanked with buttered currant bread, tiny sandwiches, unevenly shaped shortbread, a two-tier plate of scones and buttered crumpets. A marvelous warm smell of baking drifted through the air and Kirsty could see the chocolate cake was sweating slightly as the butter icing melted glassily. Her aunt shot her a wicked sidelong glance and waved to Megan before pointing to Kirsty and mouthing '*one guest for tea*'. Megan nodded, smiling, and made a note as the two joined the short queue.

Kirsty looked about her—her first impression, that the place was crowded, was a little misleading, there were only about ten others. While most were chatting with animation, at least one of the men was addressing himself to his wedge of cake with single-minded concentration. Besides the cake his small plate contained two crumpets, a scone and a shaky tower of sandwiches.

'If you eat like this all the time, I wonder you all keep your figures,' she murmured to her aunt as that masterful relative heaped their plates very nearly as high, but Edge just laughed.

'We don't eat every meal, every day, usually one, maybe two—oh, nip off and get us that sofa over there, good girl, you're quicker than me.' Kirsty nipped obediently, earning a venomous stare from a harsh-featured woman which she pretended not to see.

The dogs, she noticed, had disappeared—no doubt teatime would be far too tempting for them. She knew that Grasshopper Lawns always had a few rescue animals around, and the main house always had two resident Labradors, although the turnover was quite high as the residents tended to adopt one into their homes. At last count there had also been a donkey, a very elderly sheep, and a flock of ex-battery hens which contributed free-range eggs.

Edge broke her train of thought as she sank down next to her, with another resident, wielding a large teapot, following closely behind to serve them tea. 'But there's no denying the food here is excellent,' Edge went on as though there'd been no pause in the conversation. 'Nearly all home baking, you see. There's a light breakfast in the mornings, followed by a full cooked breakfast, so you can have either or both. Elevenses is coffee and cake, lunch is fairly hearty, then there's afternoon tea, and supper is much lighter. Savoury, sweet, savoury, sweet, savoury—a dietician might have conniptions but it's all farm produce and we thrive on it. I personally come in for breakfast every day, and I do rather like a lavish afternoon tea, where I can pick what fits best with my waistline on any particular day.'

Kirsty, aware that her aunt had been blessed with the constitution of a camel, grinned at her but she had a point. No one in the room was in danger of looking malnourished, but they looked healthy. Even the man working so single-mindedly through his enormous helping looked well-padded rather than obese. Just as she was about to ask her aunt whether this was a standard turn-out, a petite woman with beautifully frosted hair, lavish false eyelashes and talons for nails, darted into her line of vision and beamed at her in such welcome her own lips automatically twitched in response. The beam widened to embrace Edge and the tiny woman came closer.

'Not often we have the police to tea, Edge. Is this

bribery and corruption?' With a tinkling laugh the newcomer perched herself on the sofa and eyed Kirsty with bright interest. 'Don't mind me, I know you're Edge's niece. Off duty, are you?'

'Unlike you, Sylvia,' Edge said sweetly, 'you're never off duty, are you? Kirsty, my love, this is Sylvia McBain, who was a Cold War spy. Or so she tells us.'

Sylvia tittered. 'Edge, you are awfully rude. Now Kirsty, tell me all about this terrible thing. Was poor Betsy shuffled off this mortal coil, and who do we have to thank?'

'It's far too early to tell.' Kirsty said formally but added, with a touch of her aunt's gentle malice, 'however, just in case, maybe you could tell me where you've been all morning?'

'Dear girl.' Sylvia patted her lips carefully with a paper serviette. 'I don't mind at all. I've been grilled by the KGB, you know, and you are so much prettier, the image of your aunt in fact. As it happens, I was working on my memoirs. When we run out of people to tell our stories to, here, we start writing them down. So I was deaf and blind to the world, even though my apartment is two doors away from Betsy's. And in this cold weather—so like Moscow in winter—my doors and windows were locked shut. Although I did take my poodle Froufrou out for a walk about half an hour after she phoned you.'

Kirsty shot her a surprised look and Sylvia met it blandly. 'Dearest, we all know when she phoned. The bush telegraph here is very nearly as good as you find in prison. She was apparently booming away, she was the bane of Matilda's life. Matilda lives in the apartment between us, and she couldn't help but hear. The apartments are supposed to be soundproofed and I suppose they aren't bad, but Betsy had a voice like a foghorn, it cut straight through Matilda's wall. And she and I walk together every day, and she told me Betsy had been bellowing away about a policeman. Not a peep from her apartment at that point. It did take absolute ages for you to get here, we thought.'

Edge came to Kirsty's rescue with a brisk attack on Sylvia's Froufrou for messing on the path, and the sharp-eyed little woman was successfully diverted. As Edge continued on the attack she eventually hopped back to her feet and took herself away with a last rather forced laugh. Edge slid the last shortbread slices onto her paper napkin and folded it into her bag.

'Darling, we'll finish these in the apartment, shall we? It's just that I can see Jamie's come on downstairs, and Major Horace has come in, and there's absolutely no way we'll escape both of them unless we make a dash for it right *now*.' She herded Kirsty out like an animated border collie through the conservatory and out the side door, but stopped at the top of the steps, gesturing with her free arm. 'Isn't that fabulous?' she demanded, 'that view—from here you can see right across Grasshopper Lawns and over to the campsite, and just look at that sky!'

Kirsty dutifully admired the purples and mauves of the darkening sky, winter trees sketched in sharp silhouette on the Bathgate hills, and tried not to shiver—the hall had been very warm, and with the sun going the temperature on the stairs was plummeting. Edge seized her arm again and marched them both down the stairs.

'Sylvia is the most inquisitive person on the planet, but she admits it so readily, and says she can't break the habits of a lifetime at this late stage, so I find it best to just be ready for her. Best defense is a good attack, and unlike Betsy she does give up stories of her own and they're cracking ones. Probably not true, but the point is not so much having an interesting past as being an interesting person, or even just a person to whom interesting things happen. Your lovely policeman will know where to look for you, I imagine, if we go straight back to the apartment. Oh, right, he's not *your* lovely policeman. How is your lovely Rory, then?'

Kirsty flushed—Edge had never cared for Rory and just lately Kirsty was beginning to agree with her, but out of loyalty she lied that his latest job was going well and seemed to be exactly what he'd been looking for.

'Well, I'm certainly glad to hear that.' Edge said approvingly. 'There comes a time when you have to settle to one thing, and he is, what, thirty, already? Great fun singing in a band of course but after ten years you have to accept that hanging around between gigs is time that could be spent working on a future. Just in case. Now, if you'll just open up the kitchen and make us tea I'll get the lights on and the curtains drawn; it's been a lovely day but there's a definite nip in the air now.'

At first glance the apartment was a well-proportioned rectangular room generously fitted with cupboards and bookshelves. In fact the doors on the left wall weren't cupboards at all. One led into a sleeping alcove, and, through that, a walk-in box-room. Another led into the fully-fitted bathroom. Kirsty, with the ease of long familiarity, heaved on the two central cupboard doors which swung out on noiseless wheels to reveal themselves as pantry doors.

The space they enclosed held a well-planned kitchenette with sink, fridge, caravan-size oven and two hot plates, plenty of storage and even a pulley shelf suspended from the ceiling. Although Edge insisted she was no cook it was certainly possible to prepare basic meals there. These were the smallest apartments available, and usually claimed by male residents, but each came with a sheltered tiny verandah and a private raised planter, and Edge had always declared herself very comfortable.

Betsy Campbell's unit, by contrast, was the designated studio apartment, the first time Kirsty had been inside one of them—one main room divided from a well-fitted kitchen by a short passage, from which branched a walk-in wet room facing a walk-in closet. The kitchen door opened onto the covered walkway, with, beyond it, a sketchy shrubbery flanking the little service road that led to the garages and the bungalows. The main room, Kirsty remembered, had French doors opening to the gardens.

'What are the bungalows like, Aunt?' Kirsty asked idly as she busied herself making them a pot of Rooibos tea. 'I was just thinking that Betsy Campbell's place was so completely different to this.'

'The bungalows are different again.' Edge agreed. 'Bigger, and the layout is more conventional. Big lounge-dining area, one big bedroom, a conservatory running the whole length of the building at the back, and space to park your car in front. They even have tiny back gardens. They *are* nice, I've been inside a couple of them, but I don't know that I'd buy one and they rarely come up for rent.'

'I thought you said all the apartments were rented?' Kirsty brought over the tea tray and poured for Edge— lemon, no sugar—put her own onto the African walnut side table and settled into the visitor chair. She resisted the impulse to kick off her heavy official shoes and tuck her feet under her.

'The apartments are rented from the Trust.' Edge nodded. 'You can buy the bungalows. Ideal for someone like Olga, my neighbour—she bought one, and lived there for a while, but now she's moved into the studio apartment and the rent she gets for the bungalow covers her studio and occasional house meals. On the other hand there are only six bungalows so they don't come up for sale very often. One will be coming up soon, my neighbour but one, Mose McKenzie, also owned one and rented it out. He died recently so his apartment is empty, and now Betsy's, I'd better be getting myself back on the applications board. If they let in someone like Betsy there's no knowing who they'll let in next.'

'Harriet Blake, for example?' Her aunt laughed, then looked astonished when Kirsty nodded through her mouthful of shortbread.

'Oh no. That's not possible. Why, it's absolutely ridiculous! I mean I have nothing against her, she's competent and pleasant enough but—no, Kirsty, I am going to investigate this. And I am absolutely getting back on that applications board. Apart from anything else she can't work here and be a resident, that's a clear conflict of interest—'

'Whoa!' Kirsty held up a frantic hand 'Heavens, Aunt, calm down a bit! I didn't mean Harriet Blake will be moving into either of the vacant places, I just meant she told us she's on the list.'

'That's not much better.' Edge was only slightly mollified. 'Applications are checked by two members of the Trust team and one resident, and I want to find out who rubber-stamped hers.'

'She told us it was all the Trust team and five residents.' Kirsty remembered and Edge nodded and topped up both their cups from the teapot.

'There are ten people at any one time available to check applications. But they only need to be signed off by two from the Trust team and one representative of the residents, and that's why I will get involved again. It's an awful bore, which is why I gave it up, but if people like Betsy and Harriet are sneaking in under the radar then I have to step back up to the podium.'

'You owe it to Grasshopper Lawns,' Kirsty agreed solemnly, and grinned when her aunt shot her a suspicious glance.

'You may laugh;' Edge said with dignity, 'but the balance in a place like this is incredibly important. Bossy domineering people can so easily become bullies, and we're all on our own without families to step in if bullying starts. Applicants have to strike the balance between timid and overbearing, be happy on their own but not too reclusive, and of course—'

'You've convinced me!' Kirsty threw up a hand again to stop her and the discussion ended in laughter.

CHAPTER TWO

Friday – dinner with Patrick

'Well, it's definately murder.' Iain said soberly. 'She was suffocated. The SOCO found the velvet cushion that was used, and the tech guys have confirmed it. Not very nice. I also got hold of Angus's solicitor; all his money, quite a lot actually, was left to the Trust. Betty Taylor had nothing to leave, she had her own pension and a widow's pension but died owing the Trust two month's rent, I got that from the Bursar at the Trust, who ended up handling the paperwork for her. And I've left a message for Mr McKenzie's solicitor, who also handled Miz Campbell's stuff—just across in Linlithgow—so we'll find if there are any leads in either will.'

'Can I tell my aunt? She's absolutely thrilled by the whole thing, has already asked me if we've found anything out yet. And she really is very discreet, despite the way she talks. She'd never breathe a word passed on in confidence?' Kirsty asked diffidently and Iain pulled a face at her.

'Normally I'd say no, no matter how discreet she was, but you've not obviously seen the paper.' He flipped the *Chronicle* across the desk towards her. 'I bought it on my way in. Front page news. Somebody tipped them off, obviously. That Missus Blake will be having a fit.'

'Oh dear, oh dear.' Kirsty skimmed the story under the bold headline *'Pensioners murdered in their homes'*. The reporter, with modern disregard for the actual facts, had said sweepingly that a series of recent deaths should be re-examined in the wake of finding that Betsy Campbell, a popular member of the community, had been found murdered in her flat after a desperate call to the police for help.

'Cheeky bugger! She won't be the only one having a fit. We can expect a few heated phone calls from upstairs, I'm thinking. Bloody *Chronic Ill* and bloody Sandy, he hates us, never misses a dig. Amazing no one has taken a velvet cushion to *him* yet, if you ask me. Oh, you may laugh,' she glanced up at Iain severely, 'but you'll feel just the same soon enough!'

Her personal mobile phone beeped politely and she snatched it up, half expecting a call from Rory, who hadn't been in touch since they quarrelled four days earlier. She'd been exasperated when he handed in his notice at the new job because they wouldn't let him take unpaid leave to go on tour with his band, and hadn't been able to hide it.

If the tour could lead to bigger things, she'd have been able to share some of his bounding optimism, but when all was said and done, the band had been together twelve years and had managed only the tiniest of ripples in the music world. Being booked as a support act for an *X Factor* runner-up who had managed to convert fifteen minutes of fame into ten bookings across the country wasn't, in Kirsty's opinion, a breakthrough. It certainly wasn't a reason to give up the first halfway decent job he'd managed to land in all the time she'd known him. Rory had taken the huff and nothing further had been said before he left for Manchester.

Excusing herself to Iain she went outside to take the call, which was from the girlfriend of one of the others in the band. Estelle had been fully supportive and even excited, but had also heard nothing. After reassuring her that her Jason was unlikely to be besieged by groupies (Jason was balding, a mediocre guitarist, and about four stone overweight, with as much charm as musical talent, but it was touching that to Estelle he was groupie catnip) she hesitated, then rang her aunt to pass on the confirmation that Betsy had been murdered.

~~~

31

After a highly enjoyable blether on the phone with Kirsty, Edge stared unseeingly out the window at the garden, her coffee cup drooping forgotten in one hand. Murder. For all she'd said she suspected it, it was still a surprise that something so dramatic had touched tranquil Grasshopper Lawns.

She lifted the phone to call her best friend, remembered they would shortly be meeting up for their exercise class, caught sight of herself in the mirror and tutted. When Kirsty rang she'd been in the middle of attempting a fairly complicated chignon, and her shoulder-length hair was making determined efforts to escape the new style. It was usually piled in an casual bun on top of her head, or coiled into a neat chignon at the back, but with a renewed onslaught and slightly aching arms she completed the new style and pushed the last pin into place. From the front, it was nothing remarkable but from the back it looked sleek and stylish.

She was pleased with it, but the novelty of creating a hairstyle also gave her an idea and she picked up the phone again. Pressing the third speed-dial option rewarded her almost immediately with a cultured Irish accent wishing her a good morning.

'Patrick, darling! I need to pick that incredible brain of yours. Will you take me out for dinner or do you want to eat here?'

After some negotiation they agreed on a particularly good local restaurant and Edge, smiling, hung up to pull on her trainers. With a quick glance out the window, where the wind was still howling, she also took her reversible all-weather cape from its hook behind the door. It was one of the staple requirements of The Lawns that all residents—and for that matter the staff— took part in regular exercise. Edge normally went three times a week and very occasionally stayed for the second session; Fridays, with line dancing, wasn't normally her favourite but with a lavish dinner coming up, she decided to put in the extra work. She grimaced as she opened the door to the hungry wind and hurried along the walkway, her cape billowing around her as she headed towards number seven. Vivian was letting herself out as she arrived and the wind urged them on together to the main house.

They had been friends for fifty years, the friendship often spanning half a world but surviving distance, husbands and wildly differing interests and lifestyles. Vivian had, in her day, been a traffic-stopper, taller than most men, with a smile that dropped them in their tracks at twenty yards, and a hair-raising lifestyle which she had abandoned without a second thought when she married a short, stout, passionately devoted international financier. After the death of her husband at fifty, she had become placid and slow-moving, content, as she put it, to let the world turn by itself while she withdrew into a gentle twilight.

Not long after Edge applied for Grasshopper Lawns, she'd persuaded Vivian to do the same and they'd moved in within months of each other. The gentle twilight had been ruthlessly banished as Vivian was towed firmly back into mainstream life by her energetic friend. If she sighed for the lost days of reading and TV and sleeping ten hours a night she never said so, and after nearly three years at The Lawns she'd shed some of the weight inertia had slung about her hips and shoulders, and her famously dramatic cheekbones were re-appearing under her enviably good complexion. At least part of her improved health could be put down to the regular exercise, but that didn't stop her grumbling gently from start to finish. Edge couldn't pass on Kirsty's nugget of news as two of their neighbours were also forging their way through the wind towards the house, but she suspected Vivian would be perturbed rather than intrigued, anyway. Not because she had liked Betsy, just because she was a nicer person—

The workout sessions were held in the Sunday room, because it had both space and a lavish supply of chairs, but only Olga, Sylvia and Edge were left to start the extended class when the others had left. Even Harriet, one of the few who exercised to the full every day, slipped away murmuring something about work piling up, but then with all the paperwork that must follow even a routine death coming across her desk, it wasn't totally unexpected. Vivian never stayed for the extended sessions, and Edge, glancing around the emptying room, suggested spontaneously that they cancel the line-dancing for the day in favour of aerobics. Matron was having none of it, and got them firmly to work, keeping a critical eye on Edge's performance and working them harder than usual.

She walked back with her Russian neighbour Olga who, as usual, had barely broken a sweat and who was rumoured to start every day with two hours of exercise before even walking across for the class. Thirty years in Britain, most of that spent in Scotland, hadn't perfected Olga's vocabulary or done much to lighten her heavy Russian accent. As usual Edge spent more of their conversation nodding and playing the words back in her head to puzzle out their meaning, rather than responding. Today, for instance, she had, with a sidelong smirk at Edge's flushed cheeks, remarked that Matron was putting up her play.

'Upping her game?' Edge guessed, and Olga grinned.

'Da. It is that choreographer, he has put her on her—mettle?' Edge had a suspicion she was being enigmatic on purpose but didn't have time to work out what Olga could have meant by 'choreographer'—there certainly wasn't one at The Lawns. Although they usually had coffee together after an extended session, her new hairstyle hadn't survived the workout. Even if it could be revived it wouldn't be smart enough for the evening Edge had in mind. There would barely be time to grab a quick shower and phone the hairdressers if she was to catch the Lawns mini-bus as it prepared to head off to library, supermarket and town centre with the usual gaggle of shoppers.

~~~

Patrick Fitzpatrick was a well-known and popular accountant in all three small towns surrounding the restaurant, and their progress to his preferred table at the back was interrupted more than once by greetings from other diners. He was perfectly aware that Edge, looking elegant and very expensive in an absolutely simple flattering red dress, was attracting a good deal of attention and was complacent and proprietal by the time they were seated. Edge, who had over-dressed deliberately with just that result in mind, bit her lip and let him order for her, widening her eyes with admiration.

'I'm getting nervous.' Patrick said frankly when the waiter had gone. 'This must be one hell of a favour. Did I tell you that you look lovely tonight?'

'Yes, Patrick my love, you did. But I don't mind you telling me again. How's your company getting on without you?'

'Not entirely without me.' Patrick eyed the bread basket just brought to the table with an interest that explained his impressive waistline. 'I've kept my favourite clients. Like you, you know that.'

Patrick had been Edge's accountant for over fifteen years, and had been the person to recommend Grasshopper Lawns, also one of his accounts, several years earlier. He was still listed as the senior partner in his thriving accountancy practice, but had recently handed over the bulk of his accounts to his two younger partners in a first step towards retirement. Despite an appearance that made him a shoo-in every year to play

Santa for charities of his choice, he was pursued with varying degrees of determination by the widows of the three towns. He still lived in the very beautiful Georgian house he had shared with his late wife, and was excluded from moving to the retirement village by a vast and affectionate family of five children and—at last count—nine grandchildren. Edge found him good company, but had not the slightest desire to become the next Mrs Fitzpatrick. They enjoyed a friendship that was the despair of the widows, had both shared and opposing interests, and were never short of conversation.

Only when the detritus of dessert had been removed and he could sit back in his chair, breathing rather heavily and with his face a good deal redder, did he return to the original subject. 'I'm fortified now. Consider my brains at your disposal.'

'Well, my love, it's about Grasshopper Lawns. Are they also one of your favourite accounts, the ones you've kept on? I just wondered how stable it is, financially. Not for public knowledge, whatever you tell me is between us.'

'The Trust itself? I did their last audit, then handed them over to Fellowes. But I told you at the time I recommended them; the land and buildings are owned outright. There's no risk there. The five Board appointments have their salaries comfortably covered by rental income—there's no recession big enough to make you worry about your home. It can't go bust.'

'I did wonder,' Edge met his eyes directly, 'and this is

absolutely off the record, how much they rely on bequests to top up the original kitty?'

'There have been a few of those,' he agreed, 'and no Trust would ever turn them down. But the way it was originally set up, it could meet all expenses for over a year without any rental income at all. The bequests— particularly the big one from Angus Burns, which his estate paid just before the audit—have extended that to close on two years. The staff wouldn't get their bonuses, but their jobs would be safe, and all overheads met.'

'Bonuses?' Edge looked alert and Patrick sighed with pleasure as their coffees were delivered.

'This isn't exactly a secret,' he stirred his coffee delicately, then shot her a look under his brows, 'but it isn't generally bandied about either. So I'm counting on what you said earlier, about keeping this between us. The Trust staff gets paid good, but not excellent, salaries. As the Trust is a non-profit organisation, at the end of the financial year, after all expenses have been paid and the maintenance kitty topped up, anything left over goes into a bonus pot and gets divvied up between them. It's just an incentive scheme, really. You wouldn't believe how many retirement options there are out there; if people aren't happy they give a month's notice and leave. Grasshopper Lawns has a remarkably low turnover in the business, but it's a delicate balancing act to keep residents feeling safe and entertained and comfortable. If the staff, through their combined efforts, keep the place running at capacity and turning a profit, their efforts are rewarded. If people were unhappy and left, or didn't like the meals so didn't eat at the house, or the place started looking tatty and not attracting applicants, do you see? There wouldn't be profits to divide.'

Edge turned that over in her mind. 'Is there any profit to any—or all—in a high turnover of residents? Or in attracting the bequests?'

Patrick leaned back again. 'Oho, so that's it, Nancy Drew? You're playing amateur detective in the Campbell murder? No, is the answer. Bequests go straight into the Trust, they don't touch the profit and loss sheet. Refurbishing the units between residents is a cost that comes out of overheads, so it actually reduces profits. Not to mention that any rumours—let alone murder! adversely affect applications. Poor Hamish is kicking himself that he didn't start phoning his way down the waiting list before the newspaper came out. If that story gets picked up nationally, it will be a real problem for the Trust. For their sake I hope the police get this solved and the murderer behind bars as soon as possible but while the killer is out there—well, Hamish has an impossible job on his hands. Get your lovely niece on the job, eh?'

CHAPTER THREE

Saturday – Dinner and theatre

By Saturday Kirsty still hadn't heard from Rory. Her relationship with Rory had started in their mutual appreciation of his looks and had survived the antisocial hours that marked both their jobs. It wouldn't, it seemed, survive his inability to let go of a dream he should have long outgrown.

If he walked through the door now, Kirsty thought dully, and begged her to let them start over, she wouldn't do it. Edge, most annoyingly, had been right, and Kirsty realized the relationship really was over when she decided to tell her aunt what Rory was really up to, and rang her shortly before the end of her shift.

Edge, to her credit, resisted any urge she might have felt to hang out flags and instead invited her niece to go to a new play in Edinburgh that evening.

'In fact,' she said over the phone, 'there's a new restaurant I wanted to try as well, and you'll be doing me a favour because Vivian and I were going and she's apparently woken up feeling like hell this morning. I was plucking up courage to go to the play on my own and was going to give up on the dinner. Any chance you can get a lift over here? Then we can go in by taxi and have wine with dinner and I can drop you off on the way home.'

'If you wouldn't rather go with someone from the Lawns?' Kirsty asked politely and her aunt's snort rattled the telephone.

'Like who?' She demanded ungrammatically. 'Sylvia? Darling, you'll be doing me a favour and turning my evening out back into a treat.'

Less than half an hour after resigning herself to a dreary evening on her own, Kirsty was sitting on Edge's little verandah, well wrapped up against the winter chill in a pair of borrowed woollen slacks topped with a cable-knit jumper, her police uniform neatly packed in a bag, and a cup of coffee to warm her cold fingers.

'This is wonderful! And darling, I have to tell you, I've been doing a little investigating on our murder.' Edge said proudly to Kirsty, who eyed her uneasily.

'Don't do a Miss Marple on me, Aunt,' she begged. 'Honestly, that only happens in books. I'm not going to bring you our results and ask for your wise and aged

41

input, so don't even think of asking.'

'Aged input indeed!' Edge gave her a very unfriendly glance. 'And don't tell me the police don't rely on public input, because I know you do.'

'Yes we do. And you know very well I was grateful to you for that tip-off on that drug dealer who lived opposite you before you moved here. But there's a big difference between noticing something under your nose, and going looking for trouble. I am absolutely not going to encourage you to go looking for Betsy Campbell's murderer and get yourself bumped off in turn. You know you're my favourite aunt.'

'I'm your only aunt,' Edge retorted, unmollified, 'and if this isn't under my nose I'd like to know what is. I just wondered if you've found out who tipped off the papers. Because as best I can find out it wasn't one of us.'

'Tipped off the papers?' Kirsty accepted a rather lop-sided slice of gingerbread loaf, liberally buttered. 'Well, there are, what, nearly fifty people here at any one time, between staff and residents and cleaners brought in? We didn't even bother to find out, why should we?'

'Because it affected the applications list. Having a definite murder, as a result of a possible murder, in one small community—my contact said that people on the buyers list aren't picking up their options for Mose's bungalow, for example. Heaven knows what it's doing to the rentals list. What if it was somebody who wants to jump the queue?'

Kirsty looked at her aunt with affectionate

42

exasperation. 'Dearest Aunt Beulah, do you seriously want us to investigate the first, what, fifty? people on that list?'

'It wouldn't hurt to find out if people are dropping out,' Edge said stubbornly, 'and to find out what the first person to say yes was doing on that day. And in the name of all that's holy, Kirsty Cameron, don't call me Beulah!'

'I'll tell you what, I'll run it past Iain,' Kirsty promised, 'and now, I don't know if you noticed, I'm off duty as of half an hour ago and I'm here because this is my afternoon off after a terrible week and you promised me an absolutely fabulous night out and I don't want to talk about police business at all. And if that outfit hanging on the cupboard door, the green and black jersey suit, is the outfit you've put out for me for tonight I absolutely love it. In fact I love this jersey, too!' She did look very attractive indeed with her flaming hair and milky skin set off to perfection by the creamy wool and Edge told her so with proprietary pride. Not a word more was said about Rory, or murder, and the conversation turned to the slightly odd taste of the gingerbread loaf, which Edge had bought at the house.

~~~

It was one of those perfect December days which winter doles out so sparingly, and the two Camerons cut their tea short to take Vivian's dog for a walk while the light was still good, before changing for the evening.

'Aren't you two a pair!' Vivian, whose cold was expanding at a terrific rate and who was bundled up to the ears even in the warmth of her apartment, looked admiringly from one to the other in their padded Parkas and knitted hats. 'Honestly, Edge, I hate you, you could be her older sister.' Buster, an aging black Labrador, pushed gently past her with his lead in his mouth to put an end to the conversation, and led them briskly towards the road, his entire rear end stirred by his fervent tail.

'He kens his way,' Kirsty said drily as he towed them up to the pedestrian part of the top gate. She obediently pulled it open, and Edge laughed.

'He's a lovely dog, he marches Vivian all over the place. Looks like he's set his mind on the campsite today, though, that's quite a short walk. He's very protective of Vivian, probably doesn't want to leave her for too long. I thought she was making a mistake taking on one of the house's rescue dogs but he's been the most brilliant success.'

Once they were safely across the road she unclipped his lead and he charged off to investigate an alarmed quiver in some nearby gorse. Kirsty looked about with interest—although the police were called occasionally to the campsite in the height of season, it was empty now, the caravan spots untenanted and the few guest rondavels shuttered and quiet. The few shops at the top of the campsite, rather to her surprise, had their lights on.

'What, the shops stay open all year, even when the

campsite is like this?'

'Oh yes—in fact I could do with getting some more milk, we can walk up that way. Harry's team don't just rely on the campsite, most of the people on this road get their odds and ends here, it's the closest place for them. And it's the only petrol supplier for about five miles. The general shop is open all year, but this time of year, *Rainy Days* only opens at around lunchtime and they close at about five. If they could get a liquor license they'd be open every night. Come to think of it, now they'll be able to apply again through the Trust.'

'Why, what's changed? Oh, let me guess, Betsy Campbell?'

'Violently agin it, and because the whole thing is under the Trust it has to be unanimous. She stirred up a lot of feeling against it. She only ever went into our own pub to huff and puff at anyone enjoying a quiet bevvie, and rail at them about the demon drink. I told you she was totally unsuitable for this place.' Edge glanced across at her thoughtful niece and started to laugh. 'Ha, you can take the girl out of uniform but you can't take the uniform out of the girl, just look at you thinking furiously away!'

Kirsty laughed and blushed. She hung back while Edge plunged into a particularly boggy bit to recapture Buster, who was enthralled by the trembling gorse and had to be dragged away. A philosophical dog, he cast it one last longing glance before resignedly accepting his leash and walking the two up to the little row of shops. Kirsty wandered around while Edge got into an involved conversation with the proprietor, and had a quick look in *Rainy Days*.

The snooker table was hosting a desultory game but the place was otherwise empty and she roamed round with interest. A long serving counter in the main room was unmanned—by the look of it, the usual attendant was one of the snooker players. The room also offered a jukebox, magazines, newspapers, second-hand books, DVDs and comics. There was a front room for reading, a secure soft-play room and a kind of hobbies room with several tables and shelves stacked with jigsaws and games for slightly older children. The place had a cheerful, slightly raffish air and she could imagine it becoming quite popular as a family-style pub in this fairly isolated area.

As they walked back through the fast-gathering dusk they waved at Sylvia, walking with a woman Kirsty hadn't met, and a standard poodle which could only be Froufrou.

'Would you really have invited Sylvia tonight if you hadn't invited me?' she asked when they'd handed Buster back to Vivian, and made their way back to Edge's apartment.

'I suppose so.' Edge unlocked the door and let them in. 'I just don't like going out alone. Olga's English isn't up to a play, the men here would panic if I invited them or, worse, think I was interested in them, and anyway most of us are half-deaf. I can't imagine anything worse than going to a play with someone who kept asking me in a penetrating whisper what had just been said.

Sylvia's very entertaining company in small doses so, yes, she'd have been my fallback if you couldn't have made it.'

'How about your big beau, Patrick?' Kirsty hung up her borrowed parka and pulled open one of the pantry doors to switch on the kettle, and Edge shot her a concerned glance.

'I was out with Patrick last night, two nights in a row would make us both uncomfortable. Darling, do you want to go home instead? Honestly, I don't mind if you want to cancel, I don't want you to feel pressured.'

'No! No, not at all, I'd much rather be with you enjoying myself than brooding at home, I'm just a little worried—no, not worried—a little surprised. I know you have a thriving social life and I somehow got the impression that you were all madly sociable here and did everything together. So when you tell me that if Vivian's sick your best option is a woman you'd already told me you don't much like, I'm—taken aback.'

'Well;' Edge draped the green and black jersey outfit carefully over a chair, and rummaged in her wardrobe to reappear with a purple armful. 'Betsy wanted us all to be madly sociable and do everything together. Preferably with her in charge and directing all the fun. I think it's lovely that you think I have a thriving social life here, and certainly I'm lucky in that I do enjoy my life as it is. You know I travel a lot, one of the perks of being here is that I can just lock the door and go. When I am here—well, it's comfortable. If I go into our wee pub there's no one—except Major Horace, he is *such* a chauvinist—I wouldn't enjoy having a drink with. There's always someone to chat with at tea times in the hall. I genuinely like Olga, and my other neighbour is friendly, although very shy.'

She shook out the jacket of the purple outfit and eyed it critically. 'The place is sociable enough, no one would ever feel lonely because there's always something going on somewhere, especially in summer. But that's quantity. For quality, I have Vivian, and to some degree Patrick, and having lots of social acquaintances and a couple of good friends close at hand is a very comfortable place to be. Now, do you want to change in the bathroom? We've got just over half an hour before the taxi arrives, let's see if two women can get dressed and gussied up and ready to go in one small apartment on time.'

CHAPTER FOUR

Monday – tidy up for Marjorie

Buster, exhausted by his walk and muddied up to the elbows, submitted to having his legs rubbed down by Edge before loudly emptying his water bowl. He tottered through to rejoin Edge in front of the fire with a heavy sigh while Vivian busied herself in the kitchen.

Edge's fingers tingled as warmth pumped back—the morning had been the coldest so far this winter, with a mocking wind and even a dusting of icy spicules as they turned and hurried for home. Worse, she'd been lost in thought and had allowed Buster, usually so sensible, to choose a short cut through the boggiest end of the campsite and they'd both got thoroughly splashed. As warmth crept back she remembered what she'd been turning over in her mind at the time.

'Vivian,' she called abruptly, 'you wouldn't have murdered Betsy just for being annoying, would you?' There was a startled silence from the kitchen before her friend appeared in the doorway and Edge had to laugh. 'I'm not accusing you! It's—well, I don't see *why* she was murdered! I got to thinking of it on the walk. We all disliked her to some degree, but it was a passive kind of suffering for the most part. Yes, I could have strangled her once or twice, but the wish was enough.'

Vivian trundled through a hostess trolley bearing a pot of tea and all the trimmings, including several slices of home-made malt loaf. 'The way she kept on and on about me having children and wondering how I could still be here, used to make me want to smack her silly face,' she agreed comfortably. 'Help yourself, poppet, this'll get the colour back into your cheeks.' She was shaken by a bout of rumbling coughs that made her sit down abruptly, but waved off Edge's concern.

'Don't worry!' she said when she could speak again 'Matron was here this morning and left me some stuff. She's getting the doctor to call by this afternoon to decide whether I'm to move into the Frail Care until I shake this stupid cough off but really, it is getting better, this is only the second surge this morning.'

'Well, I'll take Buster in, if you have to. It'll be a pleasure. You had your 'flu shot, didn't you?'

'Of course I did, but this is my smoking legacy, I get at least a few days of bronchitis every winter, you know that. Now. Back to Betsy. You said she had a queue of people wanting to kill her.'

Edge helped herself to malt loaf. 'In one way, yes, nobody would think twice about her being murdered because she so obviously deserved to be. But being annoyed by somebody isn't really a motive, is it? I was trying to think it through before Buster led me into the bog. We're all accepting that the murderer heard her on the phone to the police saying there'd been murder done, and nipped in to suffocate her. But no one seems to know who was murdered? And also, if you think about it, Thursday was sunny but a cold day, windows and doors shut. So the only person who could reasonably have heard her is Matilda next door and I've been in Matilda's when Betsy had her TV booming away next door. You can only hear occasional words, mostly it was just a sort of whum whum whum noise which I quite agreed with Matilda was very annoying. And unless she was standing in the kitchen, no passerby in the walkway could have heard what she was saying. She's much more likely to have been on the living room phone and then nothing could have been heard from the walkway. If it was summer she might have had the French doors open but even if she did, in winter, who'd be meandering slowly by in the garden at this time of year? And then—well, we all know what she was like when she'd been having a rant. Very fired up and restless. I can't see her letting anyone in and sitting quietly down so they could suffocate her in her chair.'

'Well, that's true enough.' Vivian emptied their dregs

into the slop basin and poured out more tea. 'And she was a big woman—and very fit with all her walking and gym classes. So to hold her down with one hand and hold the cushion over her face with the other, you'd need to be bigger and stronger. That cuts out most of the residents. But you know, Edge, she did have that trick of throwing herself back in her chair and bracing herself against the arms, when she'd made a point. What if someone was in there already with her?'

'Hmm.' Edge buried her face in her cup. 'Good point. Her little victory pose. So someone could circle the chair, maybe clonk her on the head, have the cushion across her face and Bob's your uncle. Which still brings us back to who, and why. The thing is, Mose definitely wasn't murdered. I managed to pry that much out of Kirsty. Poor man had pastry flecks in his lungs and the chunk of pastry was exactly where it would be to choke him. Although it is odd he didn't buzz for help—choking isn't immediate, is it? There's a couple of minutes at least.' She gave an involuntary shudder.

'Well, if it comes to that,' Vivian said thoughtfully , 'I did hear Megan on the phone to that maintenance company, you know. She said there was a couple of panic buttons needed replacing. And that they could come anytime because the apartment was empty. I was trying to catch her attention, because I'd gone there to write into the day book that one of my plugs wasn't working and she could book it at the same time, which she did, but now that you say that, the only apartment that was empty at that time was Mose's.'

'Still, a non-working buzzer doesn't amount to murder, does it?' Edge knotted her brows together. 'You'd still need to know he was going to choke.'

'Or have a heart attack.' Vivian offered. 'He did have a dicky heart, he'd had one heart attack already. He had to be very careful.'

'But that points a finger direct at Matron or the night-nurse.' Edge's frown deepened. 'They're the only ones who'd have the run of his place.'

'Or the cleaner,' Vivian corrected her. 'Or Hamish has keys to everything. For that matter they're kept in the admin office, they're not even locked away. So that could be anyone who walked into the admin office and pinched the keys.'

'We can probably cut out the Trust staff, I had a word with Patrick and I know they actually lose out when there's a turnover in residents. The cleaners are from an agency, so they wouldn't be affected either way. And now I think about it, every apartment has three buzzers, they can't have all been broken.' She looked automatically at the panic button in Vivian's comfortable room, which winked its green light back at her. 'They've never switched mine off, for sure. And yours is working.'

'And the ones in the kitchen and bathroom.' Vivian agreed. 'I check them all the time. So, we're saying Mose was unlikely to be the murder victim Betsy was talking about.'

'Angus was more likely, but it comes down to why, again—nobody benefited directly. And it was ages ago.

Yet somehow Betsy, with her stream of questions which nobody ever answered, had decided she had enough proof of a murder to phone the police. And yes, I agree with you, the only possible answer is that there was someone with her because otherwise there wasn't enough time. You'd have to have someone listening outside the French doors, hearing enough to panic, getting invited in, calming Betsy down enough to sit her down, and all the time knowing the police could have been two minutes away and that he or she could open the door to slip out and found themselves running straight into coppers.'

'It still comes down to why. Why kill Betsy?'

'Why not?' Edge grinned at her. 'The temptation was always overwhelming! But until we know what her will has to say, we still don't have a real motive. Unless it was to do with her past. That whole warder thing, she could know something about someone who'd kill to keep her quiet. Not necessarily a resident, but say one of them had a relative who'd visited recently, and Betsy had recognized the relative as an ex-con?'

'But they'd know she'd keep quiet about it. That whole 'I cannae say and I willnae' thing, she would never be drawn on any of her experiences, she was notorious for that. She couldn't really even blackmail someone because she'd so established that *omerta* of hers.'

Edge dug into her handbag and came up with a pen and a small spiral notebook. 'I'm getting confused. Let's tackle this another way;' she scrawled a circle and wrote a large B in the centre, then draw a line out. 'Let's assume for now that Betsy was the specific target. On this line, I'm writing her past as a warder. Next motive?'

'Are we sure it was her on the phone? I mean anyone could have phoned from any apartment, and said they were her. Knowing they'd already killed her. That could completely change the time of death.'

Edge stared at her, tapping her teeth thoughtfully with her pen. 'No;' she said finally, 'Matilda definitely heard her saying the word police. She was quite taken aback, but then she heard her go back to talking normally and stopped worrying. That was why she glanced at her clock. But I'll check with Kirsty what time they logged the call, just to be sure. Nice one.' She wrote 'time' on her list. 'My fingers are still cold, I can hardly read my own writing. Anything else?'

'Her personality,' Vivian offered. 'No, don't laugh, I'm quite serious. Say her visitor had been winding her up deliberately about murders to, I don't know, scare her into leaving. Which we all really wanted her to do, let's be honest. But she over-reacted and phoned the police. Her visitor was about to be put through a fairly gruelling time and at the very least risk being charged with wasting police time, so in a fit of rage killed her.'

'Extreme, but I see your point.' Edge flashed a grin at her while drawing another line out and scratching 'personality' against it. 'So what residents can you think of who would voluntarily go into her apartment for the pleasure of winding her up?'

'Well, there it does fall down a bit.' Vivian admitted.

'She was quarrelling with half of us and the other half avoided her like the plague. Look, we need more tea, shall we move into the kitchen? The light is much better in there, too.'

Edge collected her bag and led the way through, Vivian trundling the trolley behind. Buster, ever hopeful of a walk, brought up the rear, then sighed as Edge sat and Vivian re-filled the kettle. He was returning to his bed in front of the fire in the other room when a knock at the door brought him bristling to the alert. Edge, who was nearer, got up to open it.

'Marjorie,' she said in surprise, and admitted the cleaning woman, who gave her a dentally-challenged smile and exchanged threatening glares with Buster, who hesitated, then retreated.

'Morning, Missus O,' she introduced herself to Vivian. 'I'm Marjorie, I'll be doing your cleaning for a while, anything in particular before I start?'

'Er, no.' Vivian looked bemused. 'Is Helen sick?'

'Helen's took off.' Marjorie put her bucket and tools down and started to run water into the sink. 'Got her wee inheritance, she did, and she's gone. Not seen hide nor hair of her since Thursday—didn't turn up Friday and hasn't turned up this morning.' She looked meaningfully at their cups and Edge picked up her handbag.

'Vivian, let's get out of Marjorie's way shall we? We can go back to my place.'

'Nae need.' Marjorie said gloomily. 'I can work around you ladies, nae problem.'

'Her inheritance?' Vivian had obediently picked up her handbag too, but was still looking puzzled. 'Not a close member of her family, I hope?'

'Not family at all. That Mr McKenzie from number ten, turns out he left her a nice wee giftie. Not enough to retire, we thought she was going to work on but then himself assigned her more units last Wednesday and she took the huff—turned up Thursday but never come back since. So now we're short-staffed. I've got two more units to do every week—would be three if Miz Campbell hadn't up and died. But I'll do the best job I can for you while I've got you.'

'Was Helen doing for Betsy Campbell, then?' Edge, who had been standing in a hurry-up-let's-go way at the door, looked suddenly alert and Marjorie turned to look at her.

'Aye, just started—one of her others said he wanted a male cleaner, ken. But Helen only did her once. Then she were gone, the next day I think. That were her last shift.' She lifted her soapy bucket out of the sink and put it on the floor.

'I must just go to the loo.' Vivian decided and Marjorie's face settled into lines of disapproval. Vivian hesitated, taken aback, and Edge made shooing movements with her hands.

'Marjorie was about to do the bathroom,' she explained, 'but if you're quick, it'll be fine. Won't it, Marjorie?'

A few minutes later, as they picked their way carefully along the all-weather walk which, despite all the groundskeeper's efforts, had icy patches, Vivian wheezed reproachfully, 'Marjorie could have told us stuff. You were just saying we should be looking at the cleaner, and there it turns out Betsy had just met Helen.'

'We're not asking Marjorie.' Edge said firmly. 'She's the most ghastly woman. She's been doing for me for a year and I've asked Harriet three times to switch her. I had such a nice woman before, but she retired. Now I just leave the minute Marjorie arrives, because she has an evil genius. If you want the loo, she's cleaning the bathroom. If you want a cup of tea, she's cleaning the kitchen. If you switch on the telly, she starts to vacuum. If you give up and go lie down, she wants to clean the window by the bed. And if I hadn't been there to guard the bathroom door when you went to the loo you'd have come out to find her standing waiting with her most lugubrious face right outside the door. Didn't you see her looking at our tea cups? The only way to stop her snatching them from under your nose to wash them is to offer her some too, and then she talks for bloody hours. Stands there like Mrs Mop hanging on her broom and telling you today's woes, and last week's, and if you don't shut her up she's back to the fall she had here and how she'd sue the place if she could find a solicitor to take it on, and how her stepfather beat her as a child— she's not even that good a cleaner, but at least if we clear out she'll have nothing to do but get on with her job.'

'Well, she did give poor old Buster the dirtiest look

I've ever seen.' Vivian whistled the dog back to heel as they reached Edge's door. 'But why do they keep her on if she's so awful?'

'She's honest—and reliable, even after that fall she only missed two weeks,' Edge shrugged and opened her door, 'but—well, this is Marjorie as a cleaner. She's already done my place. In her own inimitable way.'

She picked up a crumpled napkin from the table next to the sofa and lobbed it expertly into the laundry basket, which had been left outside the bathroom door. 'I'm sorry to drag you out with that cough but I'm doing you a favour. And she's self-obsessed, there's nothing she could know about Helen that you don't, if Helen used to do your place. You can tell me about her.'

'I'm not sure I can.' Vivian hung up her coat and sank into an inviting chair. Buster gave her a reproachful glance before settling himself on the hearthrug with a deep groaning sigh. 'She's been doing for me for about a year, after that Parker bloke left. She was the absolute opposite of what you're saying about Marjorie—very quiet, very quick, very efficient, even if she was busy in the kitchen when I wanted to make tea she'd whisk off and get on with something else. I preferred her to Parker, because I was convinced he nicked stuff, but she wasn't one to be drawn on anything, any chat we had was about the weather, that sort of thing. I did ask once how long she'd been with the agency and she said about four years, but just the way she said it was a conversation stopper, her face shut down. So I have no idea what she might have done before, but she looked more intelligent than you'd expect. Oh dear, does that sound awful? I can only say the first day she arrived I was taken aback that she was the cleaner. She looked more like a visitor who'd come to the wrong door. She was—did you ever see her? About forty, I suppose. Blonde hair which she wore in a bun. Sharp features, but fairly nondescript. Always arrived in a red coat with a fake fur collar, winter and summer—oh, and patent leather shoes with diamante buckles. You know the type, everyone had them back when we were girls, but nowadays they're quite unusual.'

'Oh, I've seen her!' Edge paused thoughtfully, then added milk to both their mugs and handed one to Vivian. 'And you're right, she did look like a visitor. I just assumed she was someone's niece. Unlike Marjorie, who would look like a cleaner if you met her in full evening dress,' she added unkindly. She took the chair opposite Vivian's. 'But not a big woman. I mean not big enough to overpower Betsy.'

'Still;' Vivian said stubbornly, 'it *is* interesting that she'd just been assigned to Betsy.'

'And even more interesting that she'd inherited money from Mose.' Edge sipped her coffee. 'I can't imagine any circumstances under which I'd leave money to Marjorie. And he died so recently, even if he'd left her everything he owned it'll be months before it's all settled and paid out. So why did she vanish like that? Damn, I wish there was a way of seeing his will!'

'You get on very well with the Bursar, don't you?' Vivian asked archly and Edge gurgled involuntarily. The

Trust Bursar had a definite crush on her, and hung around beaming whenever they met at one of the parties at the house. 'So, ask him. Maybe Mose kept a copy in the strongroom?'

'That's a brilliant idea.' Edge looked at her, wide-eyed. 'I've certainly got a copy of mine there.'

'Most of us probably do.' Vivian shrugged 'I know I have. They do encourage everyone to keep wills and passports and that sort of thing locked up. And it may not be as secure as a safe-deposit box at a bank, but it's much handier.'

~~~

Edge popped her head round the door of the main office, and beamed at Hamish Kirby, who looked surprised but delighted, jumping to his feet. He was a portly little man with shrewd eyes behind thick spectacles and only reached Edge's shoulder, but he bustled about getting her coffee which she accepted with an inward sigh behind a grateful simper. Three cups in one morning—

'I trust you're not looking for Harriet,' he settled back behind his desk and glowed at her. 'She's off sorting out bridging finance, you know. Could take hours.'

'No, I was looking just for you, Hamish.' Edge abruptly switched off Mata Hari as she realized what he had just said. 'Bridging finance?'

'Well, now, keep it to yourself, I shouldn't really

have said anything,' he cautioned. 'But Harriet has agreed to buy Mose's bungalow. Not an easy decision, because it forces her to take early retirement, can't have a resident on the Board, conflict of interest. And the timing was shocking, of course, all her funds are still tied up in long-term investments which only mature at the end of next year in time for her planned retirement.'

He heaved a sigh but looked, Edge thought, unrepentant. His next words explained his relief. 'The Trust guarantees we'll sell the bungalows quickly, so that estates can be settled without delay. That means anyone on the buyers list has to be able to put up finance immediately—well, the deposit in a month, and the balance in ninety days. She just never expected one to come up so soon. This appalling scandal—well. Her retirement will be a big problem for us, of course.'

'Of course,' Edge echoed and hid her smile on her coffee cup. Hamish was known as Of-Course-Kirby to the residents, and Sylvia did a wickedly funny imitation of him. 'So will you have to take on her responsibilities in the meantime? Does that mean we'll have you here every day?'

'Ha, not that I wouldn't love to be based here, but no, Harriet doesn't officially become a resident until the sale completes. Not that we won't need the whole ninety days to recruit someone else, it isn't an easy post to fill, you know that yourself. And they have to be prepared to live in the Administrator's apartment upstairs, so that does mean someone single without dependent children. And not too ambitious—we don't want someone who sees this as a step on a long ladder, we want them to stay on for at least ten years.'

'So, somebody efficient and good at their job but not ambitious.' Edge shook her head solemnly. 'You'll have your work cut out. Funny, I had the impression Harriet was well down on the list?'

'Well, she was, on the tenant list. But she was on the buyer list as well, and that's much shorter. I contacted each person in turn, and they'd all read that ridiculous article that the papers picked up and of course they weren't happy. They hedged. It was the same with the tenants list, people usually fall over themselves to take up their option when a place comes up, but this time I was well down the list before someone agreed to take on number ten, and that was with just a natural death.'

He had the grace to look slightly sheepish. 'Between you and me, Harriet wasn't terribly keen to take the bungalow—the financing, and having to take early retirement, but of course in her position—if it ever came out that one of the Trust staff had refused to take the option because of the scandal! Well, it would have looked terrible. She's been very good about it. She'll have to move out of the house apartment, of course, as soon as we find someone, and can't go into the bungalow because of the tenant, but I think I've managed to talk her into taking Betsy's apartment. It means it'll stand empty until we have our new administrator, but frankly I don't think we could have let it otherwise. Not with the murder right there on the spot!'

'Talking of the scandal;' Edge had a complicated cover story set up but Hamish, poor sweet, was being so indiscreet anyway she decided to ditch the story and creep up on her question. 'The suggestion that Mose was murdered—I've just learned that he changed his will recently, and there's the chance, well, the odd coincidence, that one of his beneficiaries has done a disappearing act?'

'One of his beneficiaries?' Hamish looked astonished. 'I helped him with the change, because of course the main part of his estate is the bungalow. And apart from bequests to a couple of major charities, which aren't going to be disappearing, ha, he left everything to his niece. It was a very simple will.'

'And you have a copy here?' Edge looked alert, and Hamish nodded.

'Yes, he ran two copies off on his printer and signed them with me and his neighbour as witnesses, and I brought the copy away with me. Ironically, only a few weeks before he died. Poor fellow, but of course he already knew by that time his heart could let him down at any moment. Who was it you meant, this beneficiary?'

'Helen somebody, his cleaner. Apparently.'

Hamish's eyebrows climbed into his hair. 'Helen Webster? Oh no, that can't be right. She's a nice enough woman and I happen to know she gets lots of tips but no, not a beneficiary. Unless of course he made a new will, but the last one was only a few weeks ago.

Anyway, not that I'm not enjoying chatting to you, because I am, but what can I do for you?'

'Oh, er, I wanted to check the expiry date on my passport. I'm planning a little trip to the sun in February.' Edge improvised rapidly and Hamish looked faintly wistful but got out his keys. The safety boxes were kept in a locked room to which, Edge knew, all the staff had keys, but Hamish was the only person who had a master key to all the boxes in case one of the residents lost their own. Friendly and unsuspicious as he had been, she didn't dare ask him to open Mose's box so she could see the altered will, but once back in her apartment she rang Kirsty in a state of some excitement.

'Yes, we know about the will.' Kirsty sounded surprised. 'Aunt, this really is none of your business and I wouldn't be telling you except that you're roaring off finding out things and I wish you wouldn't. But yes, he left five thousand pounds to his cleaner. About the same to two charities. All signed and witnessed and very straightforward.'

'Except that he didn't.' Edge insisted. 'Just to charity, and his niece. Honestly, Kirsty, there's a copy of it here, you know. And the cleaner has vanished, hasn't she?'

'Yes, she has.' Kirsty covered the phone and Edge could hear her muffled voice talking to someone else before she came back on the line. 'Aunt, are you sure about this? Mose's solicitor thought he had the only copy of the will, and there certainly wasn't a copy in Mose's apartment.'

'Well, he could have changed it without Hamish knowing, I suppose. Who were the witnesses on the solicitor's copy? The copy here was signed by Hamish and one of Mose's neighbours. That would be either Olga, my neighbour, or the guy on the other side of him, somebody Mitchell. Bruce, I think.'

'Hang on—yes, so was the solicitor's copy. Brian Mitchell and Hamish Kirby. But five thousand pounds isn't a reason to kill anyone. And she's disappeared anyway. The solicitor can't trace her. Aunt, I'm coming to visit tomorrow afternoon anyway, let me look into this and I'll bring you up to speed then?'

CHAPTER FIVE

Tuesday – Kirsty to tea

'She's definately gone.' Kirsty accepted a shop-bought muffin and a cup of tea, kicked off her shoes and tucked her feet under her in the chair. 'And once we'd got the copy from your Hamish, we showed him the one the solicitor got. He says it looks like his signature but it isn't the will he signed. So—don't spread this around too much, right, we really don't want the media getting this yet? Promise? Then we ran the name Helen Webster through the records and she died five years ago! Next stop the agency, which luckily has quite strict screening procedures, including taking fingerprints from their employees. It turns out Helen Webster is actually Helen Spencer, who did five years for forgery. I don't need to tell you which prison, do I?'

'Ouch.' Edge winced. 'So she's back to her old tricks, sets up a nice five thousand pound legacy for herself, gets assigned a new apartment to clean and walks straight into someone who knows not only who she really is but what she really is. But still—you'd think she'd just melt away and give up on the five thousand. Not murder Betsy!'

'Aye, but you're forgetting the murder Miz Campbell called us about. Helen has to have killed the old fellow in the first place. Far from fade away, she probably had some kind of run in on Wednesday with Betsy—who by the way phoned the cleaning agency on Wednesday afternoon to ask if the Trust knew they were being sent ex-cons, but went all mysterious about it, wouldn't actually name names. The woman who runs the agency said that because of that she didn't know who was being accused, as of course they don't know who gets assigned to which apartment. The whole team reported for duty as usual on Thursday, while the agency were going to double check their records and references. Sometime between signing in that morning and the team being collected that afternoon, Helen murdered Betsy and took off. The actual details—well, we've got an alert out asking for her to help with our enquiries and we'll learn the details soon enough when she's picked up. But at least that mystery is largely cleared up.'

'So I was able to help after all?' Edge asked pointedly and Kirsty grinned at her over her cup of tea.

'Iain now calls you Jessica Fletcher, and he said I can tell you things within reason, and we can both sit back and wait for you to solve our cases. And that he'll be consulting you on one or two others, but I think he was joking.'

'All very well but we haven't solved this one yet.' Edge said briskly. 'I was told very emphatically by a policeperson I trust implicitly—well, you—that Mose was definitely not murdered. Hoping for an early heart attack is one thing, and the choking was just a bonus. But Kirsty, darling, I really don't know that you—or Betsy—can call that murder. Except that I did hear something odd about the panic buttons? And I'll tell you something else, Helen, the only time I saw her, looked a bit scrawny. Betsy was a big strong woman.'

'Well, Iain isn't happy about it and neither am I. But the Trust is really on our backs to get this sorted as quickly and quietly as possible, that Hamish Kirby has been phoning to girn at us twice a day. What's worrying Iain *is* the panic buttons—' Kirsty stopped, looking guilty.

Edge fixed her with a bright eye and Kirsty shrugged. 'I really, really shouldn't be telling you this, but you'll guess it, knowing you, as soon as they bring in the new safety thing. From next week you'll be checking them on a weekly basis. Two of the three panic buttons in Mr

McKenzie's apartment apparently had to be replaced. We've spoken to the maintenance people and they said they'd definately been sabotaged. Considering it was Helen who found him dead, when she used her passkey to let herself in, it would have been logical for her to unscrew the backs, tighten the wires, screw them up again and, you're right, nobody would ever find out. But she couldn't be sure she'd be the one who found him, could she? And even odder, the main panic button was missing. The wires had been snipped through and the buzzer was gone. Nobody, at the time, seemed to think there was anything odd about that, but of course it was so obviously a natural death.'

'Real-ly.' Edge said thoughtfully. 'Well, well. That does give one furiously to think, doesn't it?'

'Well, if she did, and that's pure speculation, you realize, if she did sabotage them she may have had trouble reversing it as quickly as she hoped. Or heard someone coming when she was halfway through fixing it, so she just cut it off hastily instead.'

'Making it obvious there was something wrong with them? Oh, no. No, if someone was coming it would have been better to leave it half fixed, maybe tuck the screwdriver into Mose's hand so it would look as if he'd been fiddling with them. That's what I would have done.'

'Please don't ever turn to crime!' Kirsty begged fervently. 'Anyway, oh Jessica, how do you see Helen getting the original will?'

'Och, sweetie, that was easy. Most of the cleaners

live in town, even I used to give Mournful Marjorie prescriptions to drop off for me on her way home, so I could collect them the next day without a tedious wait at the pharmacy, before they changed things so we couldn't handle our own meds. You'll find Mose asked Helen to drop it off at his solicitor, and she steamed it open, grabbed the chance to print off an adjusted one—we tend to go out when our cleaners arrive, you know, to give them a fair run at the place—forged the signatures and then dropped it off as requested. But I didn't realize it was Helen who found him, that's thrown my theories into a muddle. I can see her jamming his panic buttons and, I don't know, leaving a plastic tarantula or something in his sock drawer to bring on a heart attack. But not being so clumsy about hiding it. When did he actually die?'

'Choked on his morning pastry.' Kirsty said succinctly. 'Helen found him at nine, when she started her shift, and the doctor they called in reckoned he'd been dead at least an hour. Megan said he never came to house breakfasts because he told her once that he's up at six and liked his morning coffee, his toast, and a pastry, in that order, and not to have to wait for it. The house only opens for breakfast at seven thirty, apparently.'

'So that would be why it was Helen who found him.' Edge said thoughtfully. 'Megan keeps an eye out and if she notices someone hasn't come in for a booked meal she gets someone to check, but if he wasn't booked for breakfasts she wouldn't worry before lunchtime. Our rent includes a daily house meal, and most of us have it as breakfast, so she'd check on me, for example, if I hadn't appeared by ten. That's very—hang on, darling, you've made me nervous.' Edge pushed the panic button on the coffee table and within seconds her house phone flashed and rang. 'Sorry, Megan love, just me being clumsy, thanks for calling!' She smiled ruefully across at Kirsty as she replaced the phone.

'Reassured? And Helen *would* have had time to pocket her unneeded tarantula.' Kirsty said drily. 'Now, are we going to see that new thriller at the Hippodrome, or are we going to sit here and continue my busman's holiday all afternoon?'

CHAPTER SIX

Saturday – Christmas market

The reindeer were making their annual pre-Christmas appearance in Onderness, so the town centre was in full swing, the weekly market far busier than usual, and an overflow of families filling the teashop, excited children piping shrilly as their exhausted parents stared dully into space. One family gathered themselves together and left just as Edge and Vivian entered. Vivian made a bee-line for the empty table while Edge went to place their orders. She joined her friend with a sigh of heartfelt relief, plonked her packages on one of the spare chairs, and flexed her fingers.

'I should never have worn these new shoes,' she groaned, 'do you think anyone will notice if I take them off?'

'You'll never get them on again,' Vivian warned, 'and if you think I'll walk with you while you're padding barefoot down the high street through the slush, you can think again. People of our age who wear new shoes, especially with heels like that, on a shopping trip, should expect to suffer.'

'They're divinely comfortable, as long as I don't walk too far in them.' Edge said defensively. 'I'll keep them for short outings until they're fully broken in. And they do wonders for my ankles.'

'Humph.' Vivian, whose ankles had long since disappeared, opened her mouth to make a tart comment but said instead, 'Oh, there's your niece.'

Edge twisted round in her chair as Kirsty caught sight of them and headed towards their table.

'Hi, Aunt, hi, Mrs Oliver. Having a—' at that moment her shoulder Airwave murmured and she tilted her head to hear better.

'Is she wearing purple?' she asked the radio, listened again, then said, 'you can't be far from the teashop, and there's two of them here.' She turned her attention to them again. 'That was good timing. I think we've got one of your lot having a senior moment.'

'Kirsty, I wish you'd call me Vivian. And those are awful.' Vivian said sympathetically. 'I remember having one at the last Christmas party. Couldn't remember which apartment I lived in.'

'That was brandy.' Edge said rudely, and smirked. 'And *that* was payback for the comment about my shoes. Can you join us, Kirsty?'

'I'd love to, but we're at full stretch today, two officers off sick and the town heaving with visitors. Oh, here we go.' A very young constable entered the tearoom, solicitously ushering an elderly frightened-looking woman in a purple hat and scarf.

'Morning, ladies, I think this lady is one of your group?'

'Nope.' Both Vivian and Edge smiled reassuringly at the frightened woman and Edge took her parcels off the spare chair invitingly, 'but if you'd like to join us for a cup of tea and relax, you'll soon get your bearings back. Tea? Or do you prefer coffee?' The other sank onto the chair obediently and tried to smile in response, her mouth trembling.

Edge got up, winced as her feet protested sharply, and said quietly to Kirsty, 'If she still can't remember anything by the time we have to leave, should we walk her to the police station?'

Both police Airwave units crackled again, with slightly more urgency than before, and Kirsty hesitated only briefly before nodding, and leaving on the heels of her colleague. Edge ordered another round of tea and scones and limped back to the table, where Vivian was relaxing their new companion with a gentle flow of chatter about the reindeer visit.

'Don't forget to tell her about the dog bed.' Edge said cheerfully and turned to her, holding her arms wide. 'This big! Vivian has a lovely dog which sheds all over my apartment so I decided to buy a dog bed for when they visit. The only one Vivian declared would be big enough was the size, I swear, of a double bed. Took both of us and the stall-holder's assistant to carry it back to the minibus, Heaven knows where we're all going to sit with our shopping bags, going back to the Lawns. We decided we needed a cup of tea before we even start thinking about that. Vivian may have to walk, her fault for picking such an enormous bed.' The lively flow had the intended effect of engaging the older woman and making her laugh. She relaxed further as she drank her tea and nibbled on a scone, even commenting admiringly as Edge brought out a hand-knitted cashmere jersey she'd bought at one of the stalls to show them both. Finally she sat back in her chair and sighed, making both women look at her expectantly.

'I'm in Onderness, aren't I?' She looked from one to the other. 'You're both very kind. That was really frightening, but I remember now. I'm here with the family, but they wanted to go to the funfair, I said I'd find a place to have a cup of tea instead. How stupid of me to go blank. Do you think they'll be worrying?'

'There are only two tea-rooms,' Vivian said reassuringly 'they'll check both before they start to worry, they'll probably arrive any minute. So you don't live in Onderness, then?'

'No, I'm from Stirling. And my daughter, the family, live in Falkirk, the grandchildren wanted to see the reindeer so we came through for the day, but the crowds are very tiring, aren't they? Are you two—er—

with the police, that they brought me to you?'

'It was your scarf and hat.' Edge told her, grinning. 'They're purple. We're at Grasshopper Lawns.' She patted her own chest, where her purple scarf was pinned in place by a neat grasshopper pin, and nodded at Vivian's purple jersey.

'Oh, of course. Purple. But I don't have a grasshopper?'

'Not everyone does,' Vivian said comfortably, 'but it is a tradition to wear a bit of purple on our outings. Just a bit of fun but very comforting, when you're in a strange place, especially if it's crowded, to see a flash of purple and realize you belong in that group, even if you can't remember for the moment who they are.'

Their companion started laughing. 'Ken, from the old purple hat joke! I get that all the time from my daughter because of this hat, but I love it. I've heard of Grasshopper Lawns, you're all eccentric geniuses aren't you? My niece handles the finances of some of the residents. Helen Spencer, do you know her?'

Vivian, sipping tea, choked and needed a few impatient thumps on the back from Edge before she dried her streaming eyes and wheezed that she was recovering. Edge frowned at her and smiled at their new friend. 'Helen, did you say? My finances are with Fitzpatrick & Fellowes but I know her by sight. Although I don't think I've seen her about lately?'

'Oh no, you wouldn't have. I'm Amelia Spencer, by the way. I should have said earlier.'

Edge performed their side of the introductions

quickly—Vivian, still wheezing, hadn't got to the point of easy speech yet—and went back on the trail.

'She can't possibly have retired, she's far too young. What's she up to now?'

'Gone abroad.' Amelia patted her lips and eyed the last scone a little wistfully. 'Very excited about it—she got a bit of a windfall and was going to blow it on a trip, said she needed a bit of a holiday. That's the best part about her kind of work, you know, she can pick up and go at a moment's notice, half the time she doesn't even tell us about it but as it happened I rang her, couple of weeks ago now it was, and she told me she was planning it. Just as well, too, as she didn't bother to tell anyone else, just took off. Very nice for her, a chance to escape the winter weather for a break.'

'Very nice.' Edge echoed. 'Where to, lucky girl?'

'Oh, somewhere in Spain,' Amelia was a little vague. 'Costa something. Sol, I think. I've not been abroad, myself, they all sound the same to me.'

'And she's enjoying it?' Vivian, still a little hoarse, re-entered the conversation and Amelia puckered her brows.

'We haven't heard from her, actually. But that's Helen for you—she went abroad for five years a while back, and we barely had so much as a Christmas card. Even married when she was over there, her name's Webster now, but it didn't take, she came back alone. She's still Spencer professionally, naturally. Used to have her own accountancy business but there was some slight misunderstanding—' she hesitated, as if belatedly aware of saying too much, and finished with some relief, 'och, there are the family now, looking for me! Ladies, this has been a pure pleasure, I'm very glad I was wearing my favourite hat and scarf today. And thank you very much for looking after me. What do I owe you for the tea and scones?'

'Oh, nonsense, always a pleasure to make a new friend,' Edge said firmly, 'and we're about to leave, keep the table, they're probably really ready to sit down for a while.'

~~~

'Where now?' Vivian glanced back at the table where their new acquaintance was listening to both grandchildren talking excitedly at once. 'Off to see the reindeer again? Or walk down to the police station?'

'Back to the minibus, of course. What a malicious streak you have! I'm not walking a single step more than I have to, I can phone Kirsty from home and tell her what we just learned. So your Helen is a bit of a con-artist, even with her own family?'

'Handles resident finances,' Vivian snorted. 'I very nearly died, my sinuses are still tea-stained. But actually I do believe the accountant part, I told you she wasn't at all your regular kind of cleaner. I would have accepted her as an accountant without question if we'd met under other circumstances.'

'A very dodgy one.' Edge hobbled gratefully up to the minibus in the supermarket parking lot, and climbed inside with a groan of relief. 'That slight misunderstanding was probably full-blown embezzlement. Do you believe in the holiday, or was that just an excuse to leave town quickly?'

'An excuse, definitely. And the very last place you'd find her is on the Costa anything. She'll have moved to England or something, and be working as a cleaner there.'

'Well;' Edge wriggled back against the comfortable car seat thoughtfully. 'It seems odd that she'd run. The whole thing is odd. Did she sabotage Mose's buzzers, then cut one of them off to make it obvious there was something wrong with them all? Let herself into Betsy's studio, kill her, which we've already agreed she probably couldn't do, being half her size—and then dash off into hiding? She's definitely about to lose her job and get into a whole bunch of trouble. In her place, what would you do?'

'Not go to the Costa del Sol.' Vivian said stubbornly. 'If there really was a windfall, which might just have been a story for the family, I'd keep it to support myself until I'd found a new set-up. And write off the inheritance as too risky to claim, and move as far away as I could, pick a new name, and get another menial job. Maybe even go back to the Helen Spencer name so at least I could claim benefits—but no, that would bring the police straight to my door. Hmm. She would have to have a National Insurance number to get a job, wouldn't she? So she'd need to buy a new fake identity, and keep low.'

'But not murder Betsy. That's always seemed so unlikely, damnit. Unless she had every intention of brazening it out, went to talk to Betsy, heard her on the phone talking about murder and panicked? Remember Betsy didn't know about the inheritance, but Helen could have thought she not only knew about it but had jumped to the conclusion Helen had killed Mose?'

'Which takes us straight back to why, oh why, was Betsy phoning the police about a murder?' Vivian said gloomily, before being shaken by a fit of rumbling coughs which left her breathless. She was still wheezing and shaken by the aftermath as the others returned in ones and twos to the van, followed last of all by Joey, groundskeeper, driver, handyman and general odd-job man.

'Ladies, gents, I've just been hearing the weather forecast.' He opened the driver's door and hung inside, his lugubrious face more doleful than ever. 'It's a shocker—very bad moon rising. Have you all got everything you'd need to get through a week of being snowed in, if it happens?'

'Never snows before Christmas,' Major Horace boomed confidently but the others started a quick rummage through their shopping bags.

'I won't have enough milk,' Vivian wheezed and Edge nodded.

'Me neither, I'll go get for us both, but I'll need your shoes?' To the vast amusement of Major Horace and Sylvia they swopped shoes and Edge, Jamie and Matilda hurried into the supermarket to stock up on basics.

81

'What a partnership, eh?' Major Horace greeted Edge as she climbed back into the minibus. 'Just been saying to Vivian here what a team you are. Couldn't wear each other's clothes, though, eh? Eh?' He slapped his knee in appreciation of his own humour, met two very frosty glances and subsided a little sulkily.

'He was rabbiting on like that all the time you were in the supermarket, it did make me think of one thing,' Vivian said quietly under the buzz of conversation in the minibus as Joey started back to Grasshopper Lawns. 'What if Helen was working with someone? Someone big enough to sort Betsy out, for a start.'

'My head hurts.' Edge said firmly. 'I'm absolutely fed up with the lot of it. Bad enough turning murderer for five thousand pounds, now you want a whole gang sharing the proceeds?'

They sat in silence for a few minutes, then Vivian said meditatively, 'There is one other possibility. That Betsy tried to blackmail Helen. And that would serve her right because she tried it once herself, you know. Blackmail, I mean.'

'Helen did?' Edge hooted. 'On you? With your spotless past?'

'Not on me, and mine isn't that spotless, you make me sound a complete prude. But don't you remember Josie suddenly telling the whole world about her sordid history? Helen found some old newspaper story about Josie and suggested she make it worth her while to keep quiet. Not as blunt as that, but I gather it was pretty clear. Typical Josie, her immediate reaction was to tell all, but she came to warn me, because of course we both had Helen as a cleaner, to lock away any little secrets that I had. It was ages ago, I'd forgotten all about it. But how ironic would it be, if she in her turn was threatened with exposure?'

'Good grief, a blackmailer with us and our hundreds of little secrets wouldn't be a good thing at all. I wonder if she tried it anywhere else? I'll have to ask Kirsty to check if she was only banged up for forgery, or whether there was blackmail in it as well, because that opens up a whole new bunch of motives. Think about it, Vivian—there's somebody with, oh, let's pick a popular one, a child pornography collection, which the computer-clever Helen finds. She's pocketing the cash and staying quiet but suddenly Betsy starts braying that she knows a blackmailer, yes she does, she'd never tell who but she knows, she knows. True Betsy style.'

'And our pornbroker thinks she knows all and silences her. Okay. That would certainly give Helen the reason to run like a hare. Her little source of income has turned to murder once, he has nothing to lose by turning to it again, that's quite good, actually. But;' Vivian was violently shaken by another coughing fit and Edge, suddenly noticing that Sylvia was listening intently, hushed her when the fit ended with an expressive roll of her eyes in Sylvia's direction. What could she have heard? Edge ran their conversation back through her head and was satisfied that their voices had dropped low enough that all Sylvia could have picked up was her own laughing comment about Vivian's spotless past. Enough to tune in her radar, to be sure, but she couldn't have heard the rest over the conversation of the others and the car radio. Not even with, Edge thought slightly maliciously, her spy training—

~~~

'Oh, Vivian;' Harriet Blake came down the stairs as the shoppers hauled their bags out of the mini-van. Joey the driver, looking like an enormous mushroom under the new dog bed, had already set off across the lawn towards Edge's little verandah. Harriet shot his departing back a sharp look, then turned back to Vivian. 'We've got a cleaner we used to have, Parker, coming back to work here. I was wondering if you would be prepared to have him back?'

'I'll have him,' said Edge firmly, before Vivian could reply 'Rather than Marjorie? Come on, Harriet, I'd take a mass-murderer sooner than Marjorie.'

'A mass—what?' Harriet looked taken aback, then smiled thinly. 'Oh. You heard about Helen's past, then? The agency were very apologetic, very apologetic indeed. So you'd be okay with having a male cleaner? I know not everyone likes that, but I think Vivian was happy enough with him, weren't you?'

'I suppose so.' Vivian bent to put down her heavy bags. 'I'm not that fussed about Marjorie.'

'Did he talk constantly?' Edge demanded with heavy irony. 'Get under your feet the whole time?' Vivian shook her head and Edge nodded at Harriet 'I want him.'

Vivian started to cough again and Harriet shot her a concerned glance. 'You sound awful, hen. Leave your bags, Joey will bring them over, just get yourself tucked up in bed and I'll ask Matron to stop by this afternoon. Get those lungs inside as fast as you can, do you want a wheelchair back to your flat?'

Vivian, still unable to speak, shook her head violently and Harriet hurried back up the stairs to go for Matron. As Edge picked up her parcels in one hand and put the other under Vivian's elbow the first lazy flakes of snow began to fall.

'So, Parker?' she prodded, as much to keep Vivian distracted as out of real interest, as they started down the covered walkway.

'Well, he pinches things, food, and bits of cash— never anything valuable, he wasn't that obvious, but leave a handful of cash lying around and you can be sure there'll be less of it when he's been. I dropped my Mont Blanc pen, a really good one, behind my chair one night and couldn't be bothered to start moving furniture at midnight. Then I forgot, and by the time I wanted to do my crossword the next night it was too late, he'd been and it was gone. I was really annoyed about that because it was a gift.'

Buster exploded from the apartment as she opened the door, and described an exuberant circuit of the lawn before finding a tatty branch and bearing it proudly back to Vivian, who started to laugh and had to brace herself against the doorframe as her cough overtook her again. 'Damn, he needs to be walked.'

'He doesn't really, we took him for a walk this morning before we went into town, remember? He just needs a comfort stop in the drying area and if you've got some baggies on you, I'll pick up after him. Harriet's right, you have absolutely got to take a break. And no, I'm not coming in, because you'll rush around being a hostess if I do. Go in, sit down, and when Buster's finished—look, he's back already. Told you. Give me the baggies and get your feet up, woman, before you do yourself a mischief.'

~~~

Once back in her apartment, and with the offending shoes thrown crossly into the back of her wardrobe, Edge couldn't settle. She dragged the new dog bed in from the verandah, found a spot for it between the visitor chair and the fire where it didn't crowd the room too much, and sat down opposite it to study the effect. Her new library books looked boring, the television seemed choked with sport and the small amount of tidying that her apartment needed only took a couple of minutes. Putting up her simple Christmas decorations— a tree with built-in shimmering lights, and a Tiffany-style mural in the window—took minutes and did nothing to make her feel less restless. Vivian, exhausted by her first outing in a week and her chronic coughing, had agreed to have a nap and Edge had promised to collect Buster after tea and walk him, but in the meantime she was completely at a loose end and not in the mood to switch on her computer and check her social media. She peered out at the leaden sky, still issuing fitful individual flakes, and grimaced. On an impulse she put on her new jersey and her cape, found her comfortable old Clarks, and strode decisively up to the house to look for company. The big hall, with lunch well over and an hour to go before teatime, was now festively decorated but, annoyingly, empty for once, and Megan was pinning up the new cleaner rota on the noticeboard. Edge came up behind her to read it over her shoulder and tutted loudly.

'Marjorie for me *again*, Megan? You know I can't stand her! I spoke to Harriet earlier, she was going to give me Parker and you've put him against Vivian. I know she doesn't care for him, can't he do for me instead?'

'Parker's agreed to come back, so we're slotting him in with his old units where we can.' Megan said patiently. 'Anyway, Edge, not me who makes the decisions. Harriet drew this up while you were all out shopping and she's not here this afternoon. You can take it up with her on Monday.'

'She's determined to leave me with Marjorie,' Edge said crossly 'I must have asked her twenty times. Is Hamish here? I'll take it up with him.'

'Hamish? He is, but it's got nothing to do with him, he has no contact with the cleaners.'

'Oh, but—oh.' Edge looked narrowly at Megan. 'Nothing to do with them?'

'Absolutely nothing.'

'I need to see him. Right away.' Edge turned on her heel, oblivious to the irritated look Megan threw at her back, and took to the stairs up to the administration floor. Hamish was, as always, delighted to see her.

'Helen Webster.' Edge said breathlessly. 'You said you knew her quite well?'

'I wouldn't say quite well' Hamish said defensively, 'but yes, she was in quite often. She had a box here.'

'I thought only residents had boxes?' Edge put a hand to her chest. The in-house exercise classes three times a week kept her fit, but running up a flight of stairs wasn't her usual *modus operandi* and her lungs were complaining furiously.

'Well, of course. But Helen was in a difficult situation, I believe she was living with a bit of a deadbeat who stole from her. She asked, and we had a box free, so I didn't see the harm, and that way she could keep her tips safe without having to bank them. I didn't see any harm in it.' Hamish repeated and Edge sat down abruptly.

'Hamish, you *have* to open that box. I know you've got keys, and if there's just money in there you'll need me as a witness, and if there's anything else we can phone the police. There are all sorts of questions about Helen and that box could have some of the answers. It could even give us a lead to who killed Betsy, but Hamish, if I'm right, there's going to be a lot of bad news in there. Bad for Grasshopper Lawns, I mean. We *have* to look at it before the police do.'

It took a lot more persuasion but finally Hamish gave in and they went into the strongroom. He lifted down a box, unlocked it and gently shook the contents out onto the table.

'The missing buzzer!' Edge reached for it but Hamish caught her hand urgently.

'No fingerprints, Edge! In fact, we should both be wearing latex gloves, I've got some of the Frail Care ones somewhere—here, put these on. Why is one of the apartment buzzers here? You knew about this?'

'I knew a buzzer was missing from Mose's apartment, the police will definitely have to see this. And look, here's a computer printout about Josie.'

'Nothing there we don't know.' Hamish creased his eyes as he read the article quickly.

'Nothing there we don't know now.' Edge corrected him absently. 'Ew, look at these—' she fanned out some well-creased photographs of two masked men wrestling—or maybe not—in bizarre leather and bondage clothing and Hamish actually recoiled slightly.

'Oh dear,' he said blankly. 'What does it mean?'

'That's what I was trying to tell you,' Edge said impatiently, attempting to sift the small pile of papers and banknotes without touching them even with her gloved fingers, 'she was blackmailing people. She tried it on Josie who, good for her, called her bluff and spilt the beans herself. Someone is paying her to keep those photos quiet. And to judge by this, Hamish, they're paying quite a lot. There's the best part of two thousand pounds here.' She nudged aside some rolled notes and made a little noise in her throat. 'I'm absolutely psychic, I said child pornography, and look, this is an article about some bloke being arrested for a huge collection of child pornography. I don't recognize the name and there's no photo. But it will be someone here, for sure.'

'But who?' Hamish stepped slightly back from the table, looking appalled. 'We'll have to give it all to the police. The scandal—the scandal will pretty much wreck the place. You know that.'

'Which is why I wanted us to look at it first.' Edge reminded him patiently. 'We'll leave the buzzer. And the banknotes, and the story on Josie. We suppress the rest.'

'Child pornography.' Hamish shook his head. 'We're not protecting anyone from being prosecuted for that.'

'It's an old article.' Edge nudged the printout gently so she could read it. 'Look at the date, twenty years ago. He's not necessarily still collecting it. Not as if Josie is still a madam, after all. But that's not the kind of stigma he could face down the way she did. I'm guessing Helen found something in his apartment to suggest he had another name, Googled it, and came up with this. We can quietly tip off the police to keep an eye on him and make sure he's keeping his nose clean.'

'But we don't know who it is?' Hamish was calming down slightly and she shrugged.

'We can find out easily enough. Helen had an apartment every day to do. I'd guess it wasn't Mose. She got her money from him a different way, so he's out. And trust me, so is Vivian, there's nothing here that could relate to her. So we just need to find out who her other three were. Like I said, that could also lead us straight to who killed Betsy.'

'Depends how far back we have to go.' Hamish bent again over the photographs, his nostrils still pinched with disgust. 'Think on, it's a good two years ago she was doing Josie's place, and here's the story on Josie. We'll have to check back. To think that one of the men here, men I've had drinks with and watched the Old Firm with, could do this sort of thing—michty me.'

Edge picked up a paperknife and used it to flip the buzzer over. The cover had been taken off, exposing three wires. 'Do you know anything about these, Hamish?'

'Yes, a bit.' He took the paperknife from her and pointed. 'The double one, that's the power one. That one's connected direct to the duty desk, and that one to Matron's pager. Out of hours the duty one buzzes through to Harriet's pager, but—that's odd—' he prodded gently with the tip of the knife and the wire bent obediently under the pressure. 'The green one goes to the duty desk, but this one's loose, barely touching. Oh, this is very bad. That would have meant the only signal would have been to Matron's pager. But look.' He touched the red wire delicately with the paperknife and it slid sideways. 'It's broken. It's supposed to be a double system, fail-proof. The green one was loose, so even if poor Mose had reached it I'm not surprised it didn't work, but the red one is actually broken.'

'I doubt it was an accident, Hamish, to be honest with you. Just the fact that it's in this box makes me doubt that. The police can find out what happened but what, Hamish, are we going to do about the porn?' She bent her gaze on him and he shook his head.

'My dear Edge, don't look at me like that. We had absolutely no right to look in this box before calling the police and I'm sorry, but it isn't our place to take anything out. All we can do is ask them to be as discreet as possible. At least we do know the worst and it's up to them to join up the dots and find out who she's been blackmailing.'

Edge sighed inwardly, but rested her hand briefly on his arm. 'I do agree, Hamish, and I think you're being very wise. I suppose we'd better phone the police now. But it seems even odder, now that we've seen the box, that Helen should have bolted without collecting her cash first. Two thousand pounds is a lot of running-away money to leave behind.'

CHAPTER SEVEN

Sunday – new tenant in number 10

Edge was up earlier than usual and made coffee instead of going straight in for breakfast, standing at the window to watch the swirling snow. It hadn't yet stopped since the first flakes the afternoon before, and seemed to be getting heavier all the time. She watched the minibus lumbering through the main gate in the distance, still capped with a neat crown of snow as it left on the church run for the devout few who weren't about to let a little bad weather stop them taking early communion. Scotland was definitely reverting to the climate of her childhood, although this time round she was less inclined to wrap up warmly and go out to catch flakes on her tongue. She did open one of the glass doors to her tiny verandah to see whether her morning ritual of sitting outside was an option, and a flurry of snowflakes danced past her to die damply in the warmth. Maybe not. She wandered through the small apartment to her utility door, which opened to the covered walkway, and was instantly intrigued by the sounds of bustle and male voices. Early on a Sunday morning it may be, but the new tenant, it seemed, was moving into Mose's old apartment, two along from hers.

She watched with interest as a series of boxes and bubble-wrapped furniture was carried up the walkway and into the apartment. There were two burly men, obviously the movers, but she was shortly rewarded with a sight of the new occupant and frowned slightly. A tall, slim, grey man—grey hair, pale skin, a charcoal grey overcoat, who looked like a clerk and not at all interesting—came out to confer over the manipulation of a particularly ungainly item in bubble wrap which was quite obviously not going to fit through the door.

'Oh, for goodness sake.' Harriet said impatiently at her elbow and Edge nearly dropped her coffee with shock. 'Edge, dear, hold onto Buster for me will you, while I get this sorted out?' Edge automatically took the lead as Harriet marched forward to direct the men through the closest service corridor to the garden side, then came bustling back. 'I'm sorry about that, but really it was just as well I was here or I think they'd have broken both the door and the piano. Men are so stubborn, they don't think around problems the way we do. Now, I wanted to ask if you can take Buster for a few days? Vivian said he'd be happier with you than going into one of the kennels but if it's a problem just say the word.'

'Of course not, I like Buster.' Edge said automatically. 'What's wrong with Vivian?'

'Well, you heard her yesterday, her bronchitis is back, and quite bad.' Harriet said briskly 'She coughed all night, apparently, and Matron wants her in Frail Care under her eye. She's moved there already—Edge, do you mind if we pop through your flat and watch the movers going in to make sure they don't damage anything?'

'Come in, come in—' Edge stepped back and Buster hurried in, heading unerringly for the dog bed she had bought at the Christmas market. Harriet unclipped his lead and strode to the verandah doors while Edge cast one last look at the heap of boxes stacked under the covered walkway and closed the utility door. A piano? Maybe not a clerk, then.

The snow obligingly paused as the piano was carried along the grassed path fronting the apartments and, under Harriet's eagle eye, was borne triumphantly over the verandah railing and through the glass doors. Edge, not sure whether Harriet would be coming back, perched on her Havana chair and stared absently out at the snow-dusted garden and her own hedge quarter, which was looking very wintry and neglected, the faded stems of begonias set at forlorn angles and only a tangle of wizened stems where her geraniums had rioted in the summer. The hedge quarters were greatly prized—hedges crossing each other in X shapes at intervals around the perimeter of the main lawn, providing not only screening from the garden but also each creating four miniature semi-private garden patios. Edge's had a bench, a bird-feeder and a birdbath, a few ancient flagstones brought from her last garden, and a profusion of herbs and bulbs; in summer it was charming. At the moment it looked—Harriet's return broke her chain of thought and she rose to offer her coffee.

'No thank you.' Harriet said briskly. 'I must get back to the house and check we're all sorted for this weather—you've heard the forecast, I'm sure, snow for at least a week? We'll be snowed in for certain. Mr MacDonald is getting in just in time, it would have been a real problem if he'd been planning to move even a day later, I think.'

'He looks like an actuary.' Edge said critically and Harriet's rather heavy features lit with a sudden gleam of laughter.

'He doesn't act like one,' she said placidly enough. 'He's a well-known set designer and choreographer. Donald MacDonald? Quite a character. I must be away, you introduce yourself when he's settled in, you should get on rather well. Thank you so much for taking Buster, Vivian will be very relieved to know he's safe with you.'

She left with a quick wave, picking her way with some care along the grassed path, which could be slippery in winter—a grid sunk into the grass protected the lawn from being worn down by the passage of feet through the year, but could be treacherous when the grass was wet, or, as it was now, under a thin dusting of snow. Edge stayed where she was, as the snow hadn't yet resumed its assault, and finished her cooling coffee. A dainty pale whippet appeared, nosed around her triangle of garden, and then relieved itself on one of her flagstones and she waited for the mysterious Donald MacDonald to clean up behind his pet. Nothing. She stood up again and peered along to his apartment just as he appeared and called to the whippet, which danced toward him obediently. Man and dog turned back to the apartment and she called out involuntarily. Both stopped and looked toward her and she gestured with her cup towards her fouled garden.

'Good morning,' she smiled. 'I don't know if you noticed but your dog—?'

'Yes?' Frosty blue eyes met hers across the few yards separating them and she waved the cup vaguely again.

'Your dog messed?'

He turned to stare at the hedge garden, then turned back to face her. 'My dear lady,' he said coolly, 'I've just moved in. I don't think the world will come to an end because of one jobbie, do you?' and with that he turned on his heel and was gone, the little whippet whisking ahead of him.

'Charming,' Edge, suddenly furious, told the space where he had been. She still had two of the biodegradable doggy bags she'd taken the day before to clean up behind Buster and stalked over to the hedge garden to do the honours, dropping the revoltingly warm and soft little parcel into one of the doggy bins half-concealed at the end of the hedge arms. Her dignified stalk back to the apartment was marred by a skid on the wet grass but it seemed no one was looking out anyway and she made it safely back into the apartment to tell Buster, who greeted her with a subdued thump of his tail, that Some People had no consideration whatsoever. And, resignedly, that she was turning into one of those old biddies who got into rages over nothing and talked to their animals.

She was still out of sorts when she left Buster in one of the kennel runs outside the house and went in for the cooked breakfast, a little later than usual, and was even more annoyed to find her favourite Sunday newspaper had been claimed by someone else in her absence. There was still a choice of three left on the table and she scooped one up at random on her way into the breakfast room.

Breakfast was her favourite meal of the day and she cheered up as she browsed through the chafing dishes, choosing kippers with a poached egg, grapefruit juice and a croissant left over from the earlier continental breakfast session. As an afterthought she added a pork sausage, planning to pop it into her bag for Buster to make up for having to wait in the kennel run. Vivian never took the breakfast option, preferring to make her own and come into the house for lunch, and his routine was being completely overturned today. Her favourite table, tucked into the corner, had been claimed by two hard-talking women and on an impulse she went through into the conservatory.

It was normally a little too bright for her in the mornings but today was pearly grey, a dusting of snow on the glassed roof further diffusing what light there was. She was the only one there and with a sigh of satisfaction made herself at home at a table under a rather magnificent potted Torbay palm to enjoy her meal and catch up on the headlines of the day.

She was deep in the tribulations of the English cricket team, which was getting trounced in South Africa, when someone approached her table, and looked up with an unwelcoming frown. One of the few advantages of being single was the luxury of a silent breakfast and the frown deepened when she realized the newcomer was Donald MacDonald. He half-turned to put his tray down on the next table and turned back, his startlingly blue eyes no less frosty than they had been earlier. Seen close up, he was better-looking than she had realized, with excellent bone structure under a much-faded tan.

'I just wanted to apologize about Odette earlier,' he said abruptly. 'By the time I'd found a bag and gone out you'd already cleared up. Thank you.'

'No problem,' she returned coolly. 'I didn't realize you had intended to do it. Next time I'll leave you to it.'

'There won't be a next time. The situation was a little unusual.' He nodded to her, picked up his tray and retreated to the far end of the conservatory with, she suddenly realized, a hint of a flounce. What her mother would have called a bit of a nancy boy, then. The thought made her smile to herself, and as she remembered the tirades she'd heard Major Horace deliver on homosexuals, the smile widened.

~~~

Vivian was awake but looking tired and drawn when she went up to see her in Frail Care and to assure her that she was looking forward to having Buster for a few days.

'Oh Edge, thank you so much.' Vivian's eyes filled with tears and she dashed them away impatiently. 'Ignore me, I'm just so tired, what a terrible night. And I really did think I'd finished with my annual bout.' A paroxysm of coughing shook her violently and she sank back against her pillows and sipped at water when it finally released her. 'Bloody bronchitis. And bloody smoking. If I could go back forty years and smack that first cigarette out of my foolish fingers, honestly. What's the gossip downstairs? Everyone talking about the snow?'

'Wouldn't know.' Edge shrugged. 'I ate in the conservatory. Had it almost to myself, but I've got one snippet, Mose's apartment has been taken, have you ever heard of a Donald MacDonald?'

'Not the choreographer? Really? Well, that *will* add a touch of glamour to the Lawns, although the Major will have a heart-attack, isn't he a bit of a poofter?'

'The Major a poofter? Or are you talking about me, which isn't very kind or very true.' The deep fruity interruption came from the entrance and Edge flinched back as she took in the vision framed by the doorway. She knew William Robertson by reputation more than by sight, although his enormous figure and striking resemblance to the Holbein portrait of Henry the Eighth made him instantly identifiable, and for the last couple of weeks he had been joining the morning workout class in a very subdued fashion. Nothing had prepared her for the sight of him in striped magenta pyjamas and for one dazzled moment she felt as once, long ago, the Tudor king's last wife or two must have felt at the sight of that immense bulk in their bedroom doorway.

'Henry the Eighth in jammies,' she put an exaggerated hand to her heart. 'Or William Robertson?'

'In the flesh,' he flashed her a charming smile, 'well, under the PJs. But available for inspection on request. Vivian and I have already been making friends, and you're Edge Cameron, and only a few people think I'm a poofter. I'll leave you to your blethering, but I thought it important to set the record straight.'

Vivian said, straight-faced, 'William is currently going through a womanizing phase. I've only been here two hours and he's already propositioned me, so you'd better watch yourself.'

'Oh, I shall.' Edge was still fascinated by the acreage of vivid pyjamas, but gathered her thoughts hastily. 'And the poofter—you may know him—we were talking about is Donald MacDonald.'

'It's true there are only one or two of them in Scotland,' William said gravely 'but as it happens I do. Anyone who keeps the kind of company I do can't always avoid them, but I've never been entirely sure about him. Why did the subject come up, are you working on a musical? He's a top choreographer, so he is, but I thought he'd retired by now.'

'He's just moved into Mose's place.' Edge explained and William surged forward into the room and sank onto a visitor chair, which creaked in protest.

'Has he indeed. Well, well. That cleaner Helen would love that. All sorts of scandal for her to get hold of. But I gather she's done a runner?'

'She's gone to Spain, we heard.' Vivian shot Edge a quick glance and raised her brows at William. 'Scandal?'

'Dinnae waggle yer brows at me, woman,' he settled himself comfortably. 'That Helen was a blackmailing besom, so she was. Tried it on me. Me! I've never hidden anything, my life is an open book. And she forced poor auld Josie into the open, but I've wondered before now if some people paid up to keep her silent. Not that Donald would, he doesnae care what people think either. Now, look what I've gone and done. Sat meself down without my sticks to get me up.'

'I was actually impressed to see you getting around without them,' Edge commented, and rose to her feet. 'Where are they, can I get them for you?'

'Or you can help me up and I can have a quick grope while you do?' William leered at her so comically that she laughed aloud and slipped easily past his huge hand as she went in search of the sticks. His matched pair of sturdy ebony walking sticks were as much a part of his public appearance as the Tudorish fringe of beard, his sheer bulk and his trademark stride. She was pleased not only to meet him but to know Vivian had entertaining company. William Robertson was a critically-acclaimed Sci-Fi writer with degrees in astronomy, physics, bio-engineering and at least two other related subjects, better known for his television appearances as a resident expert than for his books—she'd tried to read one, when she realized he lived at the Lawns, and found it bewilderingly technical. It had made her a little shy of getting to know him but it was now apparent that the man behind the expertise was relaxed and funny. Vivian was laughing and coughing in equal parts when she got back and William struggled remorsefully to his feet in a flurry of sticks and apologized for making her cough.

She flapped her hand at him and pointed helplessly at Edge, who translated; 'she doesn't mind, she's sorry for coughing, and she hopes you'll visit again.'

'Of that you may be sure,' William adjusted his grip on his sticks. 'I'm delighted to have company, and such lively company too, I'm sure when you can get out more than half a sentence at a time we'll never stop talking. I've been in Hell up here up to now—that evil woman has me on a diet and exercise regime likely to kill me.'

'That evil woman indeed!' The little Matron, who'd entered the room in time to hear this flattering description, glared up at him indignantly. 'You've lost three stone under my care, there'd have been no gallivanting around without your sticks two months ago, you ungrateful old bugger. As it is, if you keep up this progress you'll be able to complete the main workout class in a week or two, and once you're doing that you can go back to your bungalow. Unless you put back so much as a single pound, if you do I'll have you back under lock and key here.'

~~~

Edge left as Matron doled out medications and shooed William back towards his room to let Vivian doze for a while after her bad night, and made her way down the stairs to collect Buster and give him a walk and his sausage. The snow had quickened and Buster made his ablutions quickly, turning obediently for the warmth of home with none of his usual reluctance.

It was rather nice to have his rumbling snores in the background as she settled at her desk for a few hours' work and what was left of the morning flashed by as she added her daily target of one thousand words to her current script. This was always the easy part, plotting in the general storyline, before the more wearisome checking of references and research, and she was soon totally absorbed. By the time she stopped for a late lunch and looked out the window, the snow was batting against the window and had spread itself several inches deep across the gardens.

Fortunately she'd stocked up well the day before and had plenty of choice for her meal, settling finally on pita and salad with chopped cooked chicken and mayonnaise. Not, she thought with a smile, something poor William would be allowed for a while. She wondered fleetingly whether Donald MacDonald had stocked up on food but had no intention of going to find out. If he hadn't, he could take all his meals at the house until the next time the minibus was able to get out the grounds.

Buster looked wistfully at the chicken and she checked he had enough dog biscuits in his bowl—Harriet had helpfully sent across his barely-opened bag of biscuits, so he was fine for several days at least, and she knew Vivian always had a back-up supply. At worst—and the snow was only supposed to last four or five days—she'd be able to get more at the store on the campsite.

CHAPTER EIGHT

Monday - Snowed in

Harriet had amended the cleaner schedules after all; when the familiar knock came at the door it wasn't Marjorie but a sallow round-shouldered man in his forties with, Edge soon found, an inability to look her in the eye. As she was briefing him on her few particular preferences he looked at her shoulder, the ground and out the window, and she finally gave up the mild challenge of forcing eye-contact on him and whistled for Buster, who had shot off to the covered area after greeting the cleaner.

Another twenty four hours of uninterrupted snow meant it was now heaping itself even on the sheltered patios and spilling across the walkways. Buster was reproachful at again being left in a house run while she went in to breakfast. Talking to Parker, and the detour to the runs, had made her late again, and because of the weather there were more residents than usual. The breakfast room was full and even the conservatory was filling up, with empty places but no empty tables. As she hesitated in the doorway with her tray, her name was bellowed and she saw William waving to her.

With an inward sigh at the prospect of a sociable breakfast she made her way carefully to the spare seat at his table, only realizing as she sat down that Donald MacDonald, who nodded at her unsmilingly, was on his other side, concealed by his impressive bulk.

'Does Matron know you've escaped?' she asked lightly, and William gestured at his plate with a grin.

'Bread and water, no more,' he teased and Donald said drily 'Just as well you've already eaten the baked beans and black pudding.'

'Pah. Breakfast is the main meal of the day. Why, even you had sausages and scrambled eggs and look at Edge's plate, wee slip of a lass and there's enough there to feed a farmer.'

'There is not!' Edge said indignantly, then bit her lip and confessed that the pork sausages were being smuggled out for the dog.

'Seen the accident on the motorway?' William asked conversationally, then answered his own question. 'Well, even upstairs in Frail Care you can't see the actual accident but the motorway's a parking lot. A jack-knifed truck, I heard on the traffic report. Between that and this snow, cars lined up as far as you can see. There was one yellow sports job I noticed when I got up and when I'd showered, dressed and was brushing my hair it was still there. Probably hadn't moved more than ten feet.'

'I used to hate that in my commuting days.' Edge paused reminiscently in the mopping of fried egg with her forkful of toast. 'I had a short cut, a farm road that was unploughed and ungritted all winter, I'd take my life in my hands slipping and sliding to work rather than be trapped on the M9. Between the snow shovels, blankets, thermoses and the food I crammed into the car in case I did go off the road, there was barely room for my briefcase.'

'I thought you wrote TV scripts?' Donald asked, adding honey to his oat cake with a lavish hand. 'According to William, I mean. I should know by now, never listen to a Sci-Fi writer.' He glanced across with a glint of humour and Edge found herself warming to him.

'I've done most things.' She stopped, surprised, as a sudden wave of excitement ran through the room. 'Looked like a snowman;' 'trapped on the motorway;' 'wife in labour;' scraps of information were leaping from table to table but the conservatory hushed expectantly as Megan came in, looking about anxiously, then hurried over to their table.

'Donald! I know this is a silly question but did I hear correctly, that you have a kind of sleigh?'

'I do.' He raised his brows. 'Packed in my garage. Why?'

'We've just had a man walk across from the gridlock on the motorway, his wife is in early stages of labour, he's in a panic. I rang Harriet, she's stuck out there as well, she was trying to get into Edinburgh but will turn back as soon as she can get off the motorway. She said to get Joey to take Matron to the car on the quad bike but I suddenly thought if your sleigh was available, and could be attached to it, Joey could take Matron and the husband to the car, and even bring back the wife, if it seems the best solution?'

'Yes of course. I'll get it for you—it's light, but very strong.' He rose to his feet, then paused. 'How do I get to the garages from here?'

'I'll show you.' Edge pushed away the remains of her breakfast, scooped the pork sausages into her handbag in a paper napkin, and stood up. 'There's a short cut we can take, through the service entrance.'

She led the way through the busy kitchen and out the deliveries entrance, matching him stride for stride as they hurried out onto the service road. The garages lined the property boundary, out of sight of the public areas but easily accessible, each painted green with double doors secured by a simple drop lock.

'Number ten's at the end of the row. But I know mine was in the middle?' Donald stopped, puzzled, and she shook her head.

'There isn't a garage for each apartment,' she explained, 'you must be paying extra for yours. You don't remember which one it is?'

'I think—this one?' He lifted the plank away from the

EJ LAMPREY

brackets and tugged vigorously so that both doors swung silently open, crunching over the snow and revealing a tumble of boxes and, half in the shadow, a forlorn single shoe. 'No. Definately not, I don't do retro. The sixties had such hideous shoes, don't you think? It must be the next—'

'Good grief, your eyes are good! I can barely see the shoe—just that little gleam where the light caught it—and you can tell all that? Check the next garage, I'll close this one.' Edge frowned at the shoe. What was familiar about patent leather shoes with—she narrowed her eyes, yes, the sparkle in the dull morning light was a diamante buckle? She had certainly never seen it before but who had been talking about them just recently? She pulled the doors together and secured them with their plank, then hurried into the next garage to help Donald as he tenderly lifted a few boxes marked VERY FRAGILE from a rather attractive little sleigh.

'It's just the job,' he remarked as he pulled carefully on the shafts and the little sleigh moved obediently forward. 'The shafts swing together, the driver can just sit on them and the sleigh will follow.'

'Unless he bounces,' Edge said drily and Donald snorted, then held up the harness breastplate.

In less than twenty minutes the sleigh was firmly, if eccentrically, tethered to the quad bike and Joey had driven a couple of careful circles on the snowy driveway to test the connection. Matron was downstairs with blankets, a thermos and her medical bag; the young husband, still looking pinched with cold despite two hasty cups of coffee, was installed beside her in the sleigh in a borrowed anorak, and they were on the way, watched by a few inquisitive residents on their way back to their apartments. Edge and Donald, both by now well-dusted with snow, stood in the driveway until the quad bike turned out onto the road. She tilted her head up, saw Vivian's face at the Frail Care window, and waved. Vivian waved back and Edge's elusive memory suddenly popped to the surface. Patent leather shoes! Her jaw dropped involuntarily and as Donald shivered, rubbing his purpling hands together, and turned for the entrance, she caught his arm.

'Donald, wait, would you come back to that first garage with me? I've just remembered where I heard about patent leather shoes before.' She explained as they trudged back towards the garages—he had, naturally, read about the deaths and even the request for Helen to come forward for questioning—and they opened the doors again to stare down at the dusty shoe.

'Vivian said Helen wore patent-leather shoes with diamante buckles. And just one shoe, on its own, that's so bizarre?'

'And I tell you what,' he said suddenly, 'there's a bloody awful stink in here. Don't touch the shoe—'

'I wasn't going to!' she interjected indignantly as he went on, 'we'd better call the polis. Between that shoe and the mouldy smell, looks like we may have found your missing cleaner.'

~~~

Nearly an hour had passed before Detective Inspector Iain McLuskie tracked them down in the library where they had retreated to wait away from the noisy hall—many of the residents preferred to share the mild drama rather than face the near-blizzard that had replaced the lazy snow of the morning. He cocked his head in surprise as a wail echoed down the stairs.

'That's a noise I didnae expect to hear in a place like this?'

'Some woman we rescued from the motorway.' Donald put down his newspaper. 'Which is why we were looking in the garages. For my sleigh, to collect her from her car.'

'That's what I've come in for, sir.' Iain nodded at them both. 'We've got the area roped off and bin waiting for the SOCO team, but this snow's delaying everything. I've come in to apologize for keeping you waiting and to see if you'd mind hanging about a bit longer for someone to take your statements? The covered walkway's pretty much closed by the storm at this point so I really appreciate you waiting but we'll get you back to your apartments if you prefer. My superior officer from Lothian and Borders is through the worst of the traffic, it shouldn't be too much longer.'

'It's time for elevenses anyway.' Edge looked at her watch and slotted the book she had been reading back onto its shelf. 'We could grab a coffee and pastry and then go upstairs to visit Vivian and William and go over this latest development—but Iain, do please tell us, *was* it Helen in the garage?'

The DI paused, then shrugged. 'Oh aye, but don't bandy it about. Cause of death to be confirmed by the doctor, but in my unskilled opinion the knife still between her ribs had a bearing on the matter. Looks like she stumbled backwards over the boxes, shoe must have flown off, mebbe accidentally kicked by the killer while the tarpaulin was being tucked in round her. You can't see it unless both doors are pulled wide. Mind, it's no great hiding place, she could have been found by now just by the smell, tarpaulin or no tarpaulin, if we hadn't had this cold spell. So, from what you said already, you opened the wrong garage by mistake?'

'I've just moved in.' Donald nodded. 'The garages have their own numbers, which don't relate to the apartments. I knew mine was one of the ones in the middle, I opened the one next to it by mistake.'

'Which just happened to belong to Miz Campbell herself.' Iain said heavily. 'As if it wasn't all confusing enough.'

'Vivian is going to be absolutely riveted.' Edge said enthusiastically. 'Come on Donald, let's get a quick bite—I'm really starting to regret giving those sausages to Buster, I am absolutely starving. Grab some pastries, so we can go upstairs and bring her up to date.'

Iain flinched, then shrugged helplessly. 'I cannae stop you,' he conceded resignedly, 'and to be honest this development has turned the whole case upside down.'

'One minute you're looking for a murderous cleaner and the next you're thinking Miz Campbell found the body, mebbe saw the killer, rushed to phone the police, and was murdered herself before she could spill the beans,' Donald said shrewdly and a grin tugged briefly at Iain's lips.

'Sherlock Holmes *and* JB Fletcher,' he said wryly, 'I'll just be taking the rest of the day off, think on. I'd appreciate it if you didn't talk to the press but you can come up with any theories you like, I'll listen to them. Someone will catch up with you later for those statements, eh?' and he was off.

'JB Fletcher?' Donald raised his brows and Edge went a bit pink.

'My niece is in the police, and I've been allowed to get a little bit involved—she's phoned me four times already, but she's on the far side of the traffic jam, Iain's told her not to even try to get through. She's raging at missing all the excitement. But I'll tell you while we're waiting for the coffee,' she promised and, rather to her own surprise, she did.

Donald was, for a brusque man, an unexpectedly good listener and asked intelligent questions. Almost before she knew it she had poured out the entire history of the murders as she and Vivian had pieced them together so far—even about Helen's strongbox, although she refused to be drawn on the rest of its contents. By the time they made their way up to Frail Care, where Vivian, watching the police cars from the window, was almost hopping from foot to foot with curiosity and impatience, Donald knew as much as they did. William, having replaced the enormous tracksuit he had worn to breakfast with his striped silk pyjamas and a padded silk dressing-gown, was also agog to know what all the excitement and police presence was about. During the long wait he'd been brought up to date by Vivian and they'd accurately speculated that another body had been found. The two patients were brought up to date with the latest developments, which sparked a lively four-way debate and increasingly elaborate scenarios for the murder until Donald lifted his hand.

'Enough with the wild theories,' he said impatiently. 'I don't suppose any of you have paper and a pen?' Vivian glanced at Edge, who produced her notebook from the other day. He opened it expectantly, flipped through the notes she'd made, and glanced up at them, eyes gleaming.

'I don't see why, between us, we can't work it out, if we tackle the whole thing logically. What do we know? Helen was a forger, we know that. She did time for it, and she did a number on wossname's will. What else do we know, for a fact?'

'She was a blackmailer.' William said stubbornly. 'And we know that for a fact, too. Not only Josie, you heard what Edge said was in her strongbox. The bits Edge would tell us, anyway. Someone in that box murdered her.' He shot a discontented look at Edge who pretended not to see it and settled herself more comfortably in her visitor chair.

'We know the buzzers were disconnected in Mose's

apartment,' she said instead, 'and that one of them was in Helen's strongbox. And wild theories or not, that implies to me that she intended blackmail.'

'I agree,' Donald said unexpectedly, then added more cautiously, 'I agree it's a strong working hypothesis, anyway. So;' he looked at the notebook, 'we've the likelihood that Helen found the buzzers weren't working, presumably when she found Mose dead and tried to buzz for help, cut one of them off, and locked it in her strongbox. Why?'

'She had to be aware if there was funny stuff with the buzzers, Mose's will would get her looked at quite closely,' Vivian said thoughtfully. 'So she assumed foul play and yes, being Helen, took it, because it could become another source of blackmail to her.'

'Assuming again,' Donald bent a reproving look on her and William stirred restlessly.

'We have to assume, dear boy,' he said crossly, 'because Helen wasn't considerate enough to lock her diary away with her little treasures. I think she took a chance on forging the will, and next minute he's dead on the floor when she goes in to clean, and I also think that whoever fiddled Mose's buzzers was probably just starting to fix them when she walked in, and startled meaningful glances were exchanged. And knowing dear Helen as I do—did—she grabbed the first chance she could to steal a buzzer because under the circumstances it was worth the try.'

'And there you have the fiction writer.' Donald said unkindly, but Vivian shouted him down.

'No, no, I think that's very good! We never thought of that, did we, Edge, that someone could have been in there when Helen walked in? And naturally then she would think the worst.' She started to cough again and Edge handed her a glass of water.

'Okay, duly noted,' Donald turned to a fresh page in the notebook. 'Different angle. Who benefits from Mose's death? And who from Betsy's? And for that matter, from Helen's, although if she did walk in on the killer that's a given. We're trying to find anyone who overlaps. Think of one, then we'll test them against the others.'

For a moment they all went silent, then Edge gave a surprised little laugh. As the others looked at her she said slowly 'I've got someone; but it's the wildest theory so far and an absolutely ridiculous motive.'

'None so far have come up with a double motive,' William said encouragingly, but Edge still looked embarrassed.

'I'm still puzzling it through but—well, the buzzer could have worked because there was a connection, it was just a very loose one. No one would have been surprised if it didn't work, but if it did, at that time of morning, it would have only rung through to Harriet. And it was Harriet who got Mose's bungalow. And it was Harriet who will be moving into Betsy's apartment. I know it's mad, but she *is* connected to all three.'

'She couldn't know she would get the bungalow.' Vivian objected and Edge shook her head.

'I know. I said it was ridiculous. But because the

rumour broke so quickly of not one but two murders, the people ahead of her on the buyers list backed off. So the first person who said yes was Harriet. She *said* the timing was wrong, and she *said* she had to whether she wanted to or not, but if you ignore what she said, what actually happened was that she jumped the queue. And she has worked here long enough to know exactly what effect rumours would have. And she had access to the buzzers—she has access to the keys to all of our apartments. So if William is right, Harriet could have been in the apartment to reconnect the buzzers and Helen would have walked in to find her ignoring Mose's dead body while she worked on them.'

She looked at the others and shrugged. 'Assume that instead of screaming for help, Helen settled calmly for a bit of blackmail. So, wild leaps here, Harriet offers to pay her off—and remember, Vivian, Helen's aunt said she'd got a windfall, and we were puzzled because Mose's estate wouldn't have paid out for months? That could be Harriet promising to pay her. Betsy dies—and Harriet is quite strong enough for that, she's a big woman herself—and the new cleaner disappears at exactly the right moment, the cleaner who just found out her new job is with her old warder. In fact Harriet, who told the police she was furious at someone leaking the story to the papers, probably did it herself to make sure they got it. Jumps the queue and also gets Betsy's studio. And garage.'

'Okay, run with this for a moment. Why didn't she get rid of Helen's body?' Donald looked dubious. 'If she wanted to frame Helen, and yes, that was working, she needed for her never to be found.'

'But she wouldn't have been.' Vivian said thoughtfully. 'Nobody would normally have been going into Betsy's garage but Betsy, and she was dead. Once Harriet had the garage that gave her all the time in the world to move things—well, the body—out of her own garage with no questions asked. She couldn't foresee the accident on the motorway, and Donald going into the wrong garage by mistake.'

William leant forward. 'Why the sudden rush to get a bungalow? Harriet's not due to retire for what, two years? And suddenly she's nobbling buzzers and—' he stopped short, looking astonished and then indignant 'and me! She had a go at me!'

Vivian bit her lip at the look on his face but managed to ask, in a voice that wobbled only very slightly, 'how did she have a go at you?'

'She bloody did! Why do you think I'm in here? My medication stopped working and my blood pressure went through the roof, less than two months ago. If Matron hadn't found me in a little heap in my library and had me brought here and onto her hellish regime of diet, exercise and different meds, I'd be watching you lot groping around for motives from my very own fluffy cloud right now. And guess who takes delivery of all the meds since the system changed? The bloody administrator, that's who! Easiest thing in the world for her to replace my pills with Tic-tacs, then sit back and wait for my bungalow to come on the market.'

'If that's true,' Donald began, and quailed in the face of an outraged stare. 'I mean, in that case,' he amended placatingly, 'yes, your question is valid. Why would Harriet be in such desperate need for a bungalow?'

'Health?' Vivian offered. 'You can't take a place here unless you're fully mobile, self-sufficient and able to do all the gym classes and get about generally. Once you're in, they won't chuck you out until you permanently need special care, but it *is* tricky getting in. I nearly didn't make it because of this wretched annual bronchitis, I know that for a fact.'

'But she's fit as a flea,' Edge objected, then frowned. 'Come to think of it, she didn't stay for the extended class last week—first time in my experience. She always stays, every day, for the full hour. On Friday she said she was busy and had to go. I didn't think anything of it but Matron didn't look surprised—maybe she hasn't been doing the second sessions lately.'

The door opened abruptly and Matron, looking very nearly flustered, stuck her head round. 'Edge!' She gasped thankfully 'oh, and Donald too! Can I borrow you both quickly? Bit of a crisis.'

'Not the baby?' Edge rose immediately. Donald, surprisingly quick, reached the door ahead of her as Matron shook her head violently.

'The baby's fine, wee lamb, sleeping peacefully. No, it's Harriet, she's come into the San looking like death, and collapsed on the floor, and I can't lift her by myself, she's such a big woman and she's just dead weight, could you help me get her onto a bed? I think it's her heart and this dreadful snow, we'll never get an ambulance through the traffic jam—'

She hurried ahead of them to the administrator, who was pulled into the recovery position on the floor of the small waiting area, and patted her hand soothingly. 'There you go, my dear, I've got a wheelchair right here and Donald and Edge to help me get you up into it, we'll have you in a room and tucked up in two ticks, you just concentrate on your breathing.'

Directed by the competent little matron the three of them managed to haul Harriet into the chair, wheel her into an unused room and help her onto the bed. Harriet refused to lie down and was in deep distress, fighting for breath with her fists clamped to her battling chest, and Matron gave up trying to press her back against the pillows, sending Donald instead to find more pillows to prop her upright and bustling off herself to chase up the ambulance already ordered for the mother and baby.

'Edge,' Harriet gasped and rolled her eyes towards her, 'Edge, I'm dying, aren't I? Oh God. Oh, the irony!'

'It wasn't supposed to happen so soon, was it?' Edge intuited. 'How long did they tell you?'

'A year, if I - didn't stop working – because of the stress. Stress, my God! A year - at best. But if I just - retired and took things - easy, I would be – fine;' she stared at the window, then suddenly blinked and looked back at Edge.

'You – knew?'

'Well, guessed,' Edge didn't want to increase the woman's distress. ' You haven't been yourself lately.'

'If you – only knew,' Harriet gasped a mirthless laugh as Donald appeared with a mound of pillows and they built them up until she could lean slightly into their support. Her colour improved marginally as her breathing steadied and Matron hurried back in with a glass of water with two fizzing sinking tablets.

'Soluble aspirin,' she said briskly, 'better than nothing, and helps stop clotting. Is this the first time?' Harriet shook her head mutely and the Matron's attention sharpened. 'If you've had a diagnosis, or you have prescription stuff, for goodness sake tell me. Do you have any medication?'

'There are pills – in my desk drawer.' Harriet twisted slightly on the pillows and Donald lifted her legs onto the bed. 'Oh that's – better, thank you. Doctors said I - would have to look at retiring – within six months – if I wanted to reach – normal retirement age.'

'So there you were worrying about early retirement, when in fact the bungalow coming up when it did was an absolute blessing.' Matron said reassuringly. Edge and Donald involuntarily exchanged glances and when Edge looked back at Harriet she realized the woman had seen them.

'I don't think so.' Harriet closed her eyes. 'I think things will – come out the way they're – written. Edge, they know then? Your niece? She told you?'

'No, nothing. Harriet, you have to relax. Just concentrate on breathing properly.'

'Stay with her.' Matron gave up on the panic button. 'Megan can't be at the front desk. I'll go for the pills but you two, please stay with her!' She almost ran from the room leaving an awkward silence filled by Harriet's laboured breathing. The breaths became gasps instead of strangled gulps and she finally opened her eyes.

'It was such a shock – the cleaner dead – who could have done – such a thing,' she looked from Edge to Donald, and saw the knowledge in their eyes. If anything she went more pale, and seemed to shrink against the pillows. 'So you do know. I thought it would be - terrible if someone found out but in a funny way, it's a relief.'

She lowered her fists and looked at them blankly before going on haltingly. 'The breathlessness – started two, nearly three, months ago. Little spasms of pain. I had some tests done – and the doctor picked up on the problem immediately. Told me what – would happen. She said – any shocks – I might even have a heart attack – I had no idea about the attacks – how bad they would be. This is the second one.' She stopped, still staring at her fists, then unclenched them cautiously. 'I never meant – to kill anyone. You have to know that. Just – the buzzers. And switching some medication. That's – not murder.' She stopped short, glanced quickly at their faces. 'You knew about that, too? About everything?'

'Yes, we do. Betsy, and Helen, and William, and Mose;' Edge stopped as Donald touched her hand warningly. True. There might be more. 'You'll feel better if you tell us,' she said instead.

'We keep people alive, you know. That's our job. At first I thought – if we just stop keeping the residents alive and — they start dying, the place will become unpopular. People will — leave and people on the — waiting list won't take their turn, and I was fairly high on the — bungalow list. It wasn't a — great plan but I couldn't think — how else to retire early, and jump the queue to get in, without — my condition being picked up — if it wasn't a bungalow. And Mose would have died anyway. He would have been — dead long before Matron got there. I need never have — touched the panic buttons. I wish I never had. I waited, and he didn't try again — so I got dressed and went down there. Oh God.' She stopped, re-living a moment, then went on again haltingly.

'The first heart attack - was just after I — killed Helen Webster. I thought my heart had burst, the pain - was so bad. She was counting the — money, and she laughed when I asked — for the buzzer. I had taken the knife just — in case. I didn't mean to kill her but she — should have brought — the damn buzzer. It was her own fault. But when I stabbed her, she fought me — it was like I'd stabbed myself - the pain - I pushed her backwards and - staggered off to the nearest bench until I could breathe again. Then I went back to the garage, to get the money back and tidy up and - close the doors, and Betsy was there, in an absolute rage because someone - had killed Spencer — that was what she called Helen, Spencer — in her garage. She was much angrier about the garage than - the murder. She never even used it — except for storage — that's why I picked hers for the meeting. I thought it was all up, then, I told her to - tell

Megan to call the police but she loathed Megan, never had a good word for her. She said she'd call the - police from her flat and I just – followed her. Such an unpleasant woman. So cross that someone had used - her garage. She didn't even look at me, how much distress I was in, she said I should come in for a – cup of tea. She would take care of it for me. So patronizing. She thought I was in shock because of seeing the body. Always meddling and - interfering. It took a minute to - realize she didn't even suspect me – and it was the most extraordinary thing. Like a light going on in my head. I thought well, if I kill her too, I could leave Helen - in the garage until I was strong enough - to move her. And if Betsy was - murdered, well, people don't want to be in a flat where someone had been murdered. If I could even rent it - myself I'd get the garage as well, and that would give me - even more time to hide Helen's body where it would never be found. Then she would be – the obvious suspect. No one would ever suspect anyone else. And having a real murder, that would make people leave, and no one would want – to come here. So much better than – than taking any more risks with the residents who - owned bungalows, until my turn came up on the list – because the murder would scare people off, do you see? My turn would come up much - faster if there was a panic. All that went through my head in a flash while - that stupid, stupid woman was - arguing with some policeman on the emergency number and when she'd put the phone down and sat back I - walked behind her chair and clamped a - cushion over her face. Big as she was, she fought less than Helen did. It was easy. It was so easy. Even the pain stopped. As though it was meant.'

For a long moment she stared out the window, her face haggard, then rolled her head on the pillow to look at Edge. 'And then because Donald - opened the wrong garage, it's over. My pills - they're in my office, locked in my - desk, so Hamish wouldn't find them and - guess that I was sick. At least I've had the chance – to say that I'm sorry.'

'Damn! If it's locked, where are your keys?' Donald pounced on Harriet's bag, which had been dropped on the visitor chair in the room. He dumped the contents on the chair, found a bunch of keys and darted after Matron. Edge half-started after him, then went back to the bed and gingerly patted Harriet's hand

'Don't you dare die, Harriet. I mean it. What other booby traps did you set? Did you have something for all the bungalow owners, for Olga? You have to tell me.'

'I never did like you.' Harriet said drowsily. 'Funny, isn't it? You're more interested – in the residents – even now – it was just Mose's buzzers. That's not murder, even Helen agreed it wasn't, but the look - she gave me. I knew I could never – defend what I had done to – anyone else. Five thousand pounds. I would have paid it, you know, but I couldn't be sure - she would never ask for more.'

'The other bungalow owners, Harriet. The other booby traps.' Edge insisted and Harriet twitched a shoulder impatiently.

'I switched - William's medication with Mary's, in number six. That Dutch woman, I put aspirin in her - pill bottle instead of the - stuff she had. Nothing that could - kill them,' a sidelong glance, 'just make it harder for them to stay alive. I couldn't think what - to do about Keith's pills, they were - quite distinctive. Olga doesn't take - any meds. I wasn't trying to kill anyone. Just make them want to – leave. Sell their bungalows.' She looked easier, as if her confession had taken a burden off her shoulders.

In the distance Edge could hear the baby whimpering, and hurrying footsteps on the stairs, and the gathering wail of an ambulance but in the room there was only Harriet's ragged breathing. Then, very softly, she spoke again.

'Do you think they can keep my - name out of the papers? I've always had - such a very good name, you know.'

AFTER CHRISTMAS

The police didn't suppress the identity of the murderer but neither did they—at the Bursar's urgent request—volunteer it, and the media never followed up. Harriet's funeral, in the Sunday Room in accordance with her will, was well-attended if not tearful, and Hamish Kirby was briefly the administrator of the Lawns, although he wasn't able to convince Edge to join him as a temporary assistant.

~

Diligent police work identified the late Angus Burns with the paedophile report in the strongbox, and made it likely that Helen's blackmail demand had, after all, driven him to suicide. Nothing was made public.

~

One of the leather-clad men in the steamy bondage photo turned out to be Major Horace, which Kirsty, although sorely tempted, never revealed to her aunt. She was, however, fairly sure that her aunt strongly suspected it, especially after Edge announced mischievously to her niece that she'd found out who the Major's cleaner had been—and that he had, a few days before the murders, insisted on switching cleaners. The new rota had switched Helen to Betsy Campbell.

~

William's health improved by leaps and bounds—which was the disgusted way he described his latest exercise regime—and he was soon able to return to his bungalow. All the bungalow owners are restored to full good health. His extravagant flirtation with Vivian continues and is much enjoyed by both parties, and a source of constant amusement to Edge. Their little group is joined, as often as not, by Donald, whose dry wit is the perfect foil to William's grandiosity.

~

When Vivian was back in her apartment and re-united with Buster, Edge missed him so much she considered adopting a dog of her own. In the meantime she frequently joins the two dog owners on walks. William hasn't yet been persuaded to go with them.

Classic whodunits should present all the clues (and red herrings) fairly, and their authors hope readers will solve the mystery a hair's breadth ahead of the characters. Or a beat behind. The main thing is that you shouldn't be impatiently waiting for the characters to catch up or, worse, completely confused by the solution, so the nicest review you could put on a whodunit book was whether you hunted with the pack and were satisfied by the hunt.

I would dearly love a review either on Amazon, Goodreads, or your social media. I hope you'll get in touch on Twitter (@Elegsabiff) or via my Facebook page (E J Lamprey); I also have a blog at Elegsabiff.com, about life, the universe, and the occasionally alarming learning curves involved in being a writer.

All the books are available on Kindle from Amazon, and are in the slow process of going into paperback.

All authors hand out free books for reviews; in my case I prefer to send books to those who have taken the trouble to review already. Email me the link of the review you've done on any of my books that you have purchased, and I will email back the Kindle version of the book of your choice. Email addresses can change: there's a mailing list option on my website at the top of the sidebar, which will always be up to date. If you sign up you get an immediate free story from the series, and I'll keep you up to date with any special offers, freebies and promotions as they come up. That would also be the link for claiming a free book after a review.

In *Three Four Knock On My Door*, it is Sylvia's handsome devoted nephew Simon, and the enigmatic Dallas from Louisiana, with life-changing news for Vivian, who come knocking. The four amateur sleuths of the retirement village combine to solve murder in between unexpected family, winter picnics, and a new resident dog causing havoc at the Lawns.

In *Five Six Pick Up Sticks*, dating for the over-fifties is definitely a boom industry, but for some it has been a dead end, and the police want to know why. Edge is unofficially and temporarily brought onto the Force to help smoke out a ruthless killer preying on wealthy widows through the singles websites. She'll be monitored at all times, so absolutely nothing can go wrong...

In *Seven Eight Play It Straight* Edge's actress stepdaughter is performing in a successful Fringe show during the fabulous Edinburgh Festival. Long-standing hostilities are set aside when a violent and bloody killing strikes all too close to home, but the temporary truce doesn't last after Fiona accuses Edge of the murder.

In *Nine Ten Begin Again* there are, unsurprisingly, murky goings-on at the Grasshopper Lawns retirement village, back where it all began, but for once they're not getting the attention they deserve. Between Edge, to her own astonishment, falling head over heels in love, and Vivian terrifying her friends by nearly dying of pneumonia, they've definitely taken their eyes off the ball. Can the four friends settle down and get on with the job in hand in time? Well of course they can, they're old hands at this by now. But it's a close-run thing.

Nine Ten Begin Again is due for release late summer 2014.

THREE FOUR KNOCK ON MY DOOR

E J LAMPREY

CHAPTER ONE

Wednesday – collect parcels

Beulah Edgington Cameron, who had been known as Edge to her friends for over fifty years, could fairly be described as an attractive woman who spent quite a lot of time on her appearance, with generally pleasing results. On this first day in February her expensively-streaked hair was caught up in a deceptively casual topknot and her neat figure encased in a heather-mix jersey suit under a camel overcoat, just right for a crisp cold morning in Scotland. The effect was definitely marred by her stockinged feet—and the fact that she was limping painfully, and using an umbrella walking stick for support—as she made her way up the stairs of the main house at the Grasshopper Lawns retirement village.

At the doorway to Frail Care she stopped short at

the sight of Donald MacDonald, her slightly supercilious neighbour-but-one, sitting in the treatment chair and looking more than usually sardonic, while Matron splinted and bandaged his hand.

'Heavens, whatever have you been doing?' she exclaimed and he shot her an impatient look.

'Ask Missus Hobbes,' he snapped and with a twitch of his head indicated the woman wringing her hands in the corner, who was looking both distressed and slightly defiant. Edge had seen her once or twice before in the dining room, a pleasant older woman with a kind face and rather haphazard dress-sense, who had moved to the Lawns just before Christmas.

'Oh Mr MacDonald, I said I'm sorry! But I only ever let her off the lead when there are no other dogs in sight. Your dog just galloped up out of nowhere!'

'Oh.' Edge drew in a breath of understanding and eyed the other woman with more interest. 'Let me guess, you own the zoomer?'

'The—I own Maggie, if that's what you mean. But she's a bulldog cross.'

'Cross?' Donald snorted, then winced as Matron tugged at the bandage. 'She's insane, not cross.' Donald, who usually surveyed the world with an air of ironic detachment, wasn't taking the present situation at all well. Edge found herself liking him more now that his usual calm and immaculate facade was ruffled, and was a little ashamed of herself.

'She's a real problem, Clarissa,' Matron said sternly. 'This is the third time in less than two months that I've had to treat someone for a bite. You can say all you want that they are just boisterous nips but this one isn't. Donald's finger was dislocated and it's quite possibly broken as well. You realize I am going to have to report this to Katryn? We can't possibly have a dog here that attacks every other dog and, for that matter, every person who walks with a stick. I'm sympathetic to the plight of rescue dogs, you know I am, but we have to consider the Lawns first. As for you, Donald, I really would have thought you'd know better than to put your hands into a dog fight.'

'The fight was over,' Donald said drily. 'The dog turned her energies toward parts to which I am very much attached. I was trying to keep them that way.'

Edge snorted with laughter, then took pity on Clarissa's real distress. 'Couldn't you muzzle her while she's out? That would be safest.'

Clarissa half-gasped. 'If you saw what she did to the vet when he tried to put a muzzle on her—'

'Well, I can help with that,' Edge offered spontaneously. 'I had a Staffie that needed to be muzzled for the vet. In fact, I've still got the muzzle somewhere. It's very wide so with any luck it will fit her. Matron, we can at least try.'

Matron looked at Clarissa and softened, then glanced at Donald. 'If Donald reports the attack to the police, there's not going to be any trying.'

He stood up and flexed his splinted hand gingerly. 'Attacking my whippet was one thing. When I swung her up out of harm's way, that dog of yours went quite deliberately for my bits. She is a complete bampot, a very nasty piece of work indeed.'

He looked severely at Clarissa, who sat abruptly and put her hands over her face, and shook his head. 'I've got to get Odette to the vet, she might need stitching. Then Joey's taking me on to the hospital for x-rays and a tetanus shot. If Odette is more badly hurt than I realized, or if the jag really hurts;'

'Of course I'll pay for everything,' Clarissa, opening her fingers to peer through, insisted anxiously. 'Everything! Poor little Odette, she's so lovely, but you were so quick, you were hauling Maggie away almost the minute she rolled her over.'

'While you ran in the opposite direction,' he remembered and she shuddered.

'Sometimes it works, sometimes she runs after me. Usually she runs after me.'

'Well, that's true enough,' Edge offered helpfully. 'A dog will often break off a threat if it thinks it's being left behind, you know.'

'Thank you, Barbara Woodhouse. Part of the deal is you getting a muzzle on that foul animal. So what brought you panting in here, anyway?'

'Oh!' Edge glanced down at her ankle, which throbbed sharply. 'I turned my ankle, and it's really painful, so I was hoping Matron would strap it for me.'

'The Zack Blacks?' Donald asked, not unkindly, and she nodded, biting her lip. 'I thought you were giving up on them after the Burns Night debacle.'

'You said yourself how good they looked, and it was hardly a debacle, Donald, be fair. We were all a bit whisky taken, and I was far from the only person who lost my balance. I thought if I wore them every now and then I'd manage a full evening in them the next time the chance came up.'

Matron chuckled at the memory. 'Falling into William's lap isn't really falling, there was no harm done. You can't just give up on Zack Black shoes!' She ushered Edge into the chair that Donald had vacated. 'Not at that price!'

Edge shook her head. 'I picked them up for a tenner on the auction after my niece Kirsty tipped me off they

were being sent over as part of the police bundle. But—
ouch! yes, there—I may give up on them. Topple me
once, more fool you. Topple me twice—'

'Just a light sprain.' Matron decided, and reached for
a stretch bandage. 'You can switch to a tube once this
has to come off, but I'll strap it for now. Donald, either
finish your Rescue Remedy or get out. You're making
the place look untidy and Joey will be waiting for you
downstairs.' She flicked a glance up at Edge as she
started deftly strapping her ankle. 'He doesn't suffer
from shock, apparently. Or doesn't believe in Bach
remedies. Clarissa had hers but Donald knows better,
eh?'

Donald pulled a face at Edge and left obediently, but
Clarissa still hesitated. Edge smiled at her.

'I'll come up to your place as soon as I've found the
muzzle, how's that?' She stood up and cautiously put
weight on her ankle, wincing. Matron told her not to be
such a baby, found her some disposable slippers to
wear home, and waved them both out, Clarissa
solicitously offering Edge her arm to hang on to.

'No, Matron's right, I'm being a wuss but I wish I'd
had a proper walking stick in the car! This umbrella one
really isn't up to the job. Once I can get to the car,
which is at the bottom of the steps, I'm going park on
the verge right outside my door rather than walk all of
two hundred yards. Not as if I could leave the car in the
visitor parking anyway.'

'Oh, were you actually out shopping when it
happened? How *awful*!'

'Collecting a parcel, a nice short outing for the shoes,
but I ended up looking an absolute idiot.' Edge said
frankly. 'My ankle went over, both knees shot out, I
dropped my parcel—my friend Vivian, have you met her

yet? She keeps telling me I'm past the age where I can wear extravagant shoes. I'm glad she wasn't there or she'd still be laughing. And the car park was absolutely full, lots of people staring disapprovingly at the Patsy lookalike wearing cocktail heels through the slush to the post office. Now,' she finished as they reached the parking lot in front of the main building. 'Am I driving you home?'

'Oh, no, no, I have to collect Maggie. I thrust her into one of the runs and rushed up the stairs after poor Donald. I'm such a fan of his, I've had a tiny crush on him for at least thirty years, you know. I used to drag Arthur to every show he was in, we saw him three times as Kinickie in *Grease*, and we went to London to see him in quite a small role in *Cats*. I was devastated when he gave up performing for good, I thought he was world-class. He was touring as Rocky in the *Rocky Horror Show* at the time. When I realized he was living here, and still gorgeous, I could hardly wait to meet him. I didn't think it would happen like this, he'll probably never speak to me again. Do you think he'll be all right?'

'Donald's tough as old boots,' Edge was ruthless. 'He's made of whipcord and leather, and he's not usually such a drama queen. It's probably the shock; he'll be fine when he's had a chance to calm down. Especially when he realizes you're a fan, I never even knew he'd done fun stuff like *Grease*, I thought he was just known for set design and choreography. You'll have to tell me all about it but not now, my feet are *freezing*.'

She shot Clarissa a mischievous glance. 'As for your crush, um, you know they say all the best men are either married or gay? Well, Donald's never been married...'

'Oh? Ohh.' Clarissa looked thoughtful. 'Really? What

a shame! Those *eyes*.'

Edge was amused. 'Very blue, but he's a bit too chilly to be good-looking, to my mind. Which is a very unfair thing to say because I do like him. And he's not the type to hold a grudge, you'll be friends yet, dinna fash.' She opened her car door and threw the umbrella walking stick across to the passenger side. 'I'll be at yours in about half an hour. No, that'll be lunchtime, so why don't I come up for a cup of tea at around three?'

~~~

Vivian, Edge's lifelong friend and a fellow resident at Grasshopper Lawns, raised her eyebrows as Edge let her in through the garden door. The small apartment, usually presentably tidy, had half-opened boxes on every chair and table, with a scattering of objects on the floor; while the sleeping alcove, its faux cupboard doors flung wide, looked as if a hurricane had been through it. The concealed box room which opened into the alcove also had its door thrown wide, and the pattern of chaos suggested it was the source of the hurricane.

'Been having a tidy-out?' She bent at what had once been her waist to pick up a hat and put it helpfully on one of the bookshelves. A generously rounded widow in her late fifties, with a beautiful smile and the fading echo of what had been extraordinary good looks, she now enjoyed the luxury of dressing to please herself and was a bright point on this dull February day in a heavy red fleece and baggy black tracksuit pants sprigged with large orange and red peonies. Her Labrador Buster picked his way cautiously over the debris to the dog bed Edge had bought for his visits, and sank to his haunches to watch developments with interest.

'I really must, some time,' Edge said ruefully. 'I'm trying to find Bertie's old stuff. I know I kept his muzzle and I've promised to help Clarissa Hobbes with that little monster of hers. You know she bit Donald?'

'Clarissa did?' Vivian, deadpan, bent again to pick up a jersey, and shook her head as she looked round for a place to put it down. 'You must dig for things like a terrier, I can't imagine what that box-room of yours must look like.'

'Oh hush and put on the kettle, if you're staying. Clarissa probably *would* have bitten him as a way of making his acquaintance, she said she's had a tiny crush on him for years. Did you know he'd been in musicals before? And apparently quite sexy in them.'

'Heavens, yes, sex on a stick. And his voice isn't bad, with more vocal coaching he could have been really good but he didn't bother, switched to choreography rather than chase the big time. I think he found the fans a bit unnerving. He likes to keep a distance, does our Donald.'

Edge hobbled back towards the box room and Vivian, obediently pulling on the pantry doors concealing the kitchenette, gave her a sharp glance.

'What have you done to your ankle?'

Edge sighed and emerged again to tell her. Vivian was, as expected, briskly unsympathetic.

'I'm not saying they're not gorgeous, because they are, but Edge honestly, what were you thinking? They ruined Burns Night for you, admit it. And it was such a good night!'

'Oh, wasn't it? The surprise, when they had a real piper for the haggis! I hope they do that every year from now; it was so much nicer than playing a CD. And

Hamish read the ode so well, too, I go to pieces after the second verse and fall over my words, but he stuck with it all the way to the end. But be fair, Vivian, dancing is not at all a Burns Night tradition. I thought we'd be sitting round stuffed to the eyebrows with haggis and shortbread and singing traditional songs in fractured eighteenth-century Scottish. If I'd known there'd be a sudden rush to dance I'd have worn shoes I could dance in. Anyway, you've made your point. I don't believe those horrible shoes were stolen at all, I think they were handed in as weapons of foot destruction and should have been blown up. I may keep one on the mantelpiece as a reminder not to be vain.'

FIVE SIX PICK UP STICKS

E J LAMPREY

CHAPTER ONE

Tuesday – Boules tournament. Kirsty.

Detective Inspector Iain McLuskie locked his police car in front of the main house at Grasshopper Lawns and struck off across the large garden with the confident familiarity of a man who knew the place well. With several murders there in fairly quick succession over the winter he'd spent a fair bit of time at the retirement village, but things had been restfully quiet lately. It was a pleasant novelty to be visiting socially, and he looked around appreciatively at the changes the season was bringing to the Lawns.

Spring had been late arriving in Scotland this year, but was making up for lost time; an army of tulips, flaunting vivid scarlet petals, marched through the

144

borders past exhausted daffodils and crocuses, and the giant bank of rhododendrons was bulging with fat buds. Privet hedges crossed each other to make X-shaped mini private gardens at regular intervals around the perimeter of the lawn; he could see a few gardening enthusiasts already hard at work in the lovely spring weather. The sky arched blue overhead, the sun was warm on his face and the lightest of zephyrs pushed a few puffs of cloud overhead, and stirred the blossom on the fruit trees.

An indifferent gardener himself, and father to young football hopefuls, his own small garden was stripped to basics. One day, he promised himself, when he had the time, he would pop back here for gardening ideas. In the meantime, he was making his way to number twelve of the apartments that encircled the lawns, to run a proposition past Sergeant Kirsty Cameron's slightly eccentric aunt Edge.

The aunt in question, who in his opinion looked ridiculously young to be living in a retirement village, was found busily weeding her hedge garden, which contained an elegant old bench and some ancient flagstones nostalgically imported from her previous home. She was wearing faded jeans, an overlarge plaid shirt and a completely disreputable gardening hat, and was clearing weeds between the flagstones with vigour and a running muttered commentary.

'I hope there aren't any swearies in that lot, Miz Cameron?' He hailed her cheerfully and she twisted round.

'Detective Inspector McLuskie! What a surprise. And of course there were swearies. Along with a magic spell that apparently banishes creeping buttercup. If it works I shall rent myself out for gardening services and be rich for life.' She used the bench's sturdy support to scramble to her feet and looked past him, surprised. 'Where's Kirsty?'

'Helping out in Grangemouth for the next few days.' He pointed at his cheek. 'You've—er—got a bit of mud...'

'Oh, I must look like hell. Gardening doesn't suit me.' She pushed her battered gardening hat up her forehead—adding two more smears of mud, to offset the rakish dab on her cheek—and shot him a sharp look. 'Not that I'm not pleased to see you, but what brings you here? Come on over to my verandah, do. I've some lemonade there in the shade.'

Two Havana chairs flanked a tiny table which held a jug of iced lemonade and a glass, and she waved him to one of the chairs.

'Help yourself, I'll get another glass. I'll only be a moment.'

He started a polite demurral but she fixed him with another sharp glance, said 'Nonsense!' and vanished inside.

Smiling, he poured himself a half-glass. Kirsty Cameron was in her twenties, a pleasant and competent police officer who was a pleasure to work with, but she was the image of her aunt. He had a sudden impression of what she would be like in thirty years' time. Still slender, still attractive, redoubtable...

Edge reappeared without her hat and gardening gauntlets, her mischievous face free of smudges, and a fresh glass in her hand. She sank down into the other chair with a sigh of relief and he held the jug up invitingly, and filled her glass at her nod.

'I hope I'm not interrupting?' He drank gratefully— the lemonade was icy, clean and sharp, delicious—and she grinned at him.

'Not at all, I was clearing my decks for Kirsty's visit this afternoon. What can I do for you?'

'I ken Kirsty visits Tuesdays so I wanted to speak to you first. I was going to ask how you were but I can see you're back to your old self, right enough.'

'Just a small operation.' She was dismissive. 'Part of growing older, such a bore, but I hope you got my thank you note for the flowers; it was very kind of you all. And being called JB Fletcher did wonders for my ward cred!'

'Ah, now, you know we value your detective skills. In fact, I'm hoping you might be interested in—well, if you're not too tied up with anything at the moment— you've jokingly said a couple of times in the past that you wanted to join the Force?'

'You're offering to sign me up as a hobby bobby?' She leaned forward, eyes bright with interest and he waved his free hand vaguely.

'Not sign up, not as such. More if you'd put in an occasional...let's call it appearance, on our behalf? I don't know if Kirsty has said anything at all about some deaths we've recently picked up on which have aroused our suspicions? I'll let her fill you in, but long story short, there's a potential link to the dating agencies that cater to singles over fifty.'

He half-filled his glass again and sat back. 'You ken the whole Scottish police force has been reorganized, aye? There's no denying that doing away with all the little divisions has improved our overall picture, and now we've picked up some odd similarities in a few geographically-scattered deaths. I'll have to ask you not to talk about it the noo, we dinnae want to start any kind of panic in case it's pure coincidence. We've been lucky; there was already a fraud investigation starting in the senior singles scene, with a top undercover poliswoman assigned to it. She's just the person to take it up a level. Problem is, all this extra information got dumped on her, and all urgent, and she says there's a limit to what she can do without ever meeting the marks. It would really help her if there was someone doing the social, appearing as her, but only in low risk situations. And it would be good to have someone— er—'

'Old?' Edge offered helpfully and he laughed awkwardly.

'No, no! I was trying to think how to say someone who could genuinely be interested in meeting senior singles. Old wasn't the word I wanted!'

'I know what you mean. Someone older, who really could be expected to want to pick up sticks and sympathize about gout. I joined one of those senior dating websites myself, once. You wouldn't believe some of the responses I got—from all ages, too. Still, it was cheap; you get what you pay for. I did think of going for one of the more expensive select introduction ones, mainly because my accountant Patrick looked on the verge of being snapped up by one of his widows, and that would have left me without my standby escort. Then he managed to escape, and I also made friends with Donald and William, so I never bothered.'

Iain grinned involuntarily. 'Life must have been very quiet before yon Laurel and Hardy! There's nothing for them in this set up, though. What I thought was, mebbe you'd like to pop round, have a talk with Susan, weigh each other up and see if it would be something that would interest you? She's working from her home, it's just over the way, in Onderness. She'll talk you through what she's doing, the possibles she's already identified, how she's monitoring things. She's very good, and a nice person, you'll like her. And you'll ken why I'm asking, when you see her. You look very like the profile picture of herself that she's posting on the websites.'

~~~

Edge poured the last of the lemonade into her glass and gazed thoughtfully into space after Iain's departure. Murder. Back in December, when Betsy Campbell's death had started a whole train of events, proximity to murder had been quite exciting, but there had been rather too much of it since then. Still, this wasn't on the spot, and her involvement would be very limited. It wasn't even confirmed that murder was involved at all—

Her train of thought was abruptly interrupted by the sight of a sizeable rump reversing slowly into view on hands and knees from the miniature garden next to her own and a breathless voice calling her name.

Stifling a laugh, she hurried over to help Miss Pinkerton up. The older woman, her neighbour in number thirteen and known to all as Miss P, gasped out grateful thanks as Edge helped her to her feet.

'Ay do it every time!' Miss P puffed ruefully. 'Ay think Ay can manage on my weeding stool, and then Ay reach too far for a pesky herb and the next thing Ay know Ay'm on all fours again. Ay don't know how you manage to get up and down so easily.'

'I don't at all,' Edge assured her. 'If it wasn't for my bench I couldn't get up either. You should get a bench in your bit, they're very useful.'

Miss P was at least seventy, with a fresh complexion, fluffy white hair and the wide candid eyes of a young girl. Writing an endless stream of wistfully romantic novels kept her in comfortable circumstances, and Edge considered her an ideal neighbour—quiet, gentle and unsociable. Over the three years they had been neighbours, Miss P's extreme shyness had only slowly thawed to the point where conversation occasionally slid past the briefest of friendly greetings, towards the first glimmerings of friendship.

'Ay really should be doing this at midnight anyway,' she said diffidently and unexpectedly. 'Dark moon, you know. Most efficacious. But at my age, midday will have to do, Ay can't be crawling on all fours to my apartment at midnight. What would my neighbours think?'

'Well, this neighbour would be quite startled, certainly. I was going to ask if you're a good witch, but even in my head it sounded exactly like a line from the Wizard of Oz.'

'Oh, not a witch at all, not really. Not any more. Ay was quite the Wiccan in my younger years, even now Ay observe the more practical rituals, like cutting herbs according to the moon phases, but Ay don't like to talk about it—or be talked about, if you'd be so kind.'

'Of course not, although I think it's fascinating. Did you at least get all your herbs?' Edge fought to rid her mind of an image of her portly neighbour dancing round a midnight bonfire, and succeeded.

Miss P beamed at her and held up a slightly crumpled woven bag. 'Oh yes, once Ay was down there Ay got the lot before Ay called for you. Ay had a feeling you'd understand when Ay heard what you said to that nice-looking policeman. Before you moved away, of course. Not that Ay would have listened if Ay...' She gave up on her jumble of sentences and settled instead for. 'Will you join me for a quick cup of tea?'

'I'd have loved to.' Edge had to shake her head. 'My niece will be here in less than an hour and I've still to make myself and the apartment presentable. Are you coming up to watch the boules later this afternoon?'

'Ay hadn't planned—well, maybe. Ay don't really go out in public alone but Ay suppose it isn't really public. That's at the top bit, where the new allotments are?'

'No need to go alone, we'll knock on your door on the way past.' Edge was firm. 'You'll like Kirsty, she's lovely. And boules is such fun.'

'It was very popular in France, when Ay lived there, but of course it was only older people who played it in those days.' Miss P seemed completely unaware of possible irony. 'Ay do remember Godfrey saying the first tournament was very successful. Did you play?'

'No, I couldn't at the time, I'd just had my op. Pity, because I love it, I've played it a bit in the past. I think the competition will be fierce today, but every time I thought I'd pop up and get in a little practice there've been people working on their game. Sylvia and Matilda are there half the day, every day. I imagine they'll be the winners today.'

'Oh, Sylvia!' Miss P permitted herself a tiny unladylike snort. They agreed she'd be ready for three thirty and she headed back to number thirteen, while Edge hurried into her own apartment to shower off the morning's exertions. She shook her head as she went. The most unlikely witch in the world, living right next door; bet that wasn't on her application form! On the other hand, the Trust only selected residents with interesting pasts, so anything was possible...

SEVEN EIGHT PLAY IT STRAIGHT

E J LAMPREY

CHAPTER ONE

Fiday – Fiona's show

Miss P leaned forward, her plump cheeks pink with excitement, to look past William and Vivian at Edge, sitting further along the row of seats. 'Ay'm so looking forward to this, Edge, Ay can't tell you how much.'

Edge shrugged helplessly. 'Remember, there'll be foul language,' she warned, for at least the third time, and Miss P giggled and put her hands up to her ears, middle fingers bent forward, to show she was ready to plug them.

'Dinna fash, me darling,' William patted her knee reassuringly. 'You'll be fine.' He patted Vivian's knee for good measure and grinned at Edge. 'We won't melt.'

'We might.' Vivian looked around slightly despairingly. 'I'd forgotten Fringe theatres are practically unventilated.'

153

'Which is why I told you to bring a fan,' Edge reminded her bracingly. She sat back and closed her eyes. It had seemed a good idea, before she left for her holiday in Florida, to buy ten tickets to this one-woman show at the Edinburgh Festival but she was already regretting it, not least because she was still slightly jet-lagged and woefully short on sleep. She and Vivian were both claustrophobic, and the theatre had been adapted from a conference room by draping it with fabric which cut out air, light and seemed to be inching in on them . . . a gentle breeze, from the edges of Vivian's fan, revived her slightly and she opened her eyes as a single spotlight sprang to life and revealed Fiona Bentwood standing a few feet away.

The show was slick, professional, bitingly funny and full of what were known locally as swearies. She did shoot one anxious glance across Vivian's agitated fan at Miss P, who was sitting with her hands in her lap and her mouth open—with any luck, she didn't know the actress's frequent drawled 'fahk' even was a swearie—but for the rest gave herself up to the performance. It was, she was relieved to realize, good. It would do well. They all applauded enthusiastically at the end and Fiona, coming forward for a bow, looked her straight in the eye and nodded slightly.

Vivian was away like a runner hearing the gun as the lights came up and Edge resisted the impulse to bolt after her and instead brought up the rear of the group, all easily spotted in the milling throng because of their purple peaks. Purple was a standing joke at the Lawns, but a flash of it was very useful in crowds, and Vivian was an ideal assembly point as she waited outside, vivid in scarlet tunic and slacks which clashed bracingly with her peak. The friends exchanged rueful glances as the group re-formed.

'Edge, I'm so sorry, this wretched claustrophobia, I couldn't bear it another minute. Did she see you? Did she come over to say hello?'

Fiona Bentwood arrived with perfect timing to answer the question herself. 'I did see her, and I've now come over to say hello. How are you, Aunt Vivian? You're looking incredibly well. Hello, Edge. You look very tired. And all of you wearing purple peaks, how quaint—are you part of a religious order, or just all from the old age home?'

'Darling. You were very good indeed.' Edge, slim, casually elegant and self-possessed, leaned forward and they air-kissed politely. 'People, this is James's daughter, Fiona. My stepdaughter.'

'My word, that makeup is jolly good,' Miss P said with wide-eyed innocent malice. 'You looked so much younger on stage!'

'Fiona, darling, this is Titania Pinkerton, you used to love her books,' Edge said hastily, and Fiona's delicate over-plucked brows twitched back from their frown.

'I still do, when I have time,' she said cordially, and shook hands. 'They're just right for someone on the road, very relaxing.' Miss P beamed, malice forgotten, and Edge went on with the introductions.

'William Robertson's also a well-known writer, although I don't know if you're into Sci-Fi? And the ballerina Olga Petrotchovitch;' Fiona twitched slightly impatiently and Edge gave up on details. 'Clarissa, Jayenthi , Brian, Matilda, Sylvia, Donald,'

'Donald MacDonald,' Fiona interrupted her, and took Donald's unresisting hand between both of her own, smiling up into his blue eyes. 'I'm a fan. Don't tell me you're at the Home too, you're never old enough! Are

155

you working on anything for the Festival? Are you still designing sets? What did you think of our set?'

'Very minimalist,' he said drily, ignoring her other comments. 'But ideal for the show. I agree with Edge, it was good. Have you been doing it long?'

'We first aired it in Grahamstown, this is the fourth Festival now, and the second year. I'm glad you liked it.' He looked bored and she relinquished his hand reluctantly to look back at William, easily the biggest man on the square—height, breadth and curving bay window. 'And I know you by reputation. My brother buys your books the minute they're published, and shuts himself away to read them. He and his partner have booked to hear you speak tonight. Are you also at the Lawns?'

'We're all from the *old age home*,' Sylvia was seething. 'Edge dragged us along to give you a bit of an audience.'

'Well, luckily you weren't the only ones here, but I do appreciate your sacrifice.' Fiona's eyes sparkled as she summed up her tiny, bristling, beautifully-dressed opponent. 'I didn't mean to offend anyone but my stepmother with that comment, and that's a battle that has raged for years.'

'True enough. And much enjoyed by all the onlookers,' Vivian said peaceably, and Fiona switched tack with a slight sneer.

'Quite the talented group, Edge, how on earth did you get them to let you in?'

'No doubt on the strength of having a famous actress as a stepdaughter, although I had never heard of you myself,' Sylvia was no Miss P, to be easily placated. 'Edge, why didn't you tell us you were related, when you invited us?'

'In case the show was awful, of course.' Edge smiled sweetly at Fiona. 'I didn't want my connections to get me evicted.'

'Oh, ha-ha.' Fiona's brows twitched back together. She was of medium height, bone thin, with delicate mobile features and a mop of unruly hair. In direct sunlight the heavy stage makeup reversed the youthful effect of the friendly spotlights and she looked older than her stepmother. 'This has been lovely, catching up, but I do have to go. Do you expect me and Jamey to visit while I'm here?'

'It would be lovely if you did,' Vivian answered hastily for Edge. 'You must be incredibly busy. I didn't realize JJ was here as well.'

'He and Tim are living back in Edinburgh, I'm staying with them during the Festival. We'll see what we can do. I know he would love to meet William.' She put the slightest emphasis on the last, swept them all with a glance and a nod which warmed to a smile as it reached Donald, and half-raised her hand in farewell before turning on her heel.

'Ooh, take that.' Sylvia was still waspish as Fiona crossed the emptying square back towards the makeshift theatre. 'You must have been a very wicked stepmother, Edge.'

'Was there ever a stepmother who wasn't?' Edge remarked lightly. 'Especially one not that much older than her stepchildren.'

The distant boom of the one o'clock gun from the Castle galvanised them into action; it had already been arranged that everyone would buy whatever they fancied from the vast variety of street stands, and head for the Princes Street Gardens to meet up for an al fresco lunch.

Clarissa tucked her hand in Edge's arm. 'Your stepdaughter looked as if she wanted to drag Donald away and eat him,' she said slightly disapprovingly, making her laugh. Clarissa had a long-standing crush on Donald which dated back to his performing days over twenty years earlier. He had moved to the Lawns shortly before Clarissa herself, and Edge, for her part, had at first thought him a chilly and unlikeable addition to the retirement village. A flurry of murders at the Lawns had proved excellent ice-breakers and she and Vivian had forged strong friendships with both Donald and the flamboyant William, but she still couldn't see what it was about him that made Clarissa so tongue-tied in his presence that she'd had to ask Edge to get Donald to autograph her cherished publicity photos from his tours with *Grease* and the *Rocky Horror Show*; or be so convinced that he had any interest in women at all. She glanced across as he and Brian, who were meeting the minibus at the Gardens, strode away and couldn't resist teasing.

'Look at the difference between the way they walk,' she challenged and Clarissa looked reproachful.

'Of course he's graceful, he was a dancer. How else could he walk?'

'You'll never convince Edge, she *insists* that he is her token gay friend.' William grinned down at them and offered Vivian his arm. 'If I faint with hunger, my lovely, you'll never get me back on my feet. I've invited Miss P to come lunch-hunting with us but if you don't stop blethering right now and feed me I'll give up on you and elope with her.' Miss P giggled and tucked a plump hand in his other elbow and Vivian patted his arm soothingly.

'Shush, William, Edge has been back two days

already and we've not had a minute to catch up. You and Miss P elope, if you feel you must.'

'No, go!' Edge shooed her with her free hand. 'We'll not all get into one taxi anyway. I promise, coffee and a long blether after exercise class tomorrow. Deal?'

Vivian eyed her narrowly, then broke into her beautiful smile. 'Deal.' She let William and Miss P sweep her away and Edge and Clarissa followed Jayenthi Pillay, who was delightedly taking photographs of a police box which looked as if it had escaped from an old Dr Who set.

Edge obligingly photographed her standing in front of it and handed the camera back. 'Shall we find a taxi and go straight to the Mound? There are always lots of food stalls and the bridge crosses the Princes Street Gardens, couldn't be handier.'

'Oh, I had hoped we would walk!' Jayenthi was wistful. 'I have friends arriving to stay this afternoon who will expect me to show them round and I have never been to the Festival before, I thought maybe you could point out a few things first —is it too far?'

Edge hesitated. 'It's pretty far for Clarissa.' However, slightly to her dismay, Clarissa, who was well into her sixties, plump and not long recovered from a stroke, felt she could manage if she could lean on Edge's arm; and said she too had never been to the Festival and would love to see it with a native. Never an enthusiastic pedestrian, especially on crowded city pavements, Edge resigned herself to the inevitable.

ABOUT THE AUTHOR

Elizabeth (E J) Lamprey lives on the Firth of Forth, within easy distance of Edinburgh, and only a few miles from where Grasshopper Lawns would be if there was a Grasshopper Lawns retirement village.

Originally from South Africa, she's the daughter of a Scot, looks like a Scot, dearly loves Scotland, but accepts that with a mere thirteen years residence she is still considered a tourist, albeit a tenacious one.

She has been variously a book reviewer on a city paper, a columnist in a national magazine, a copy-editor and critiquer, a commercial blogger, and a reporter on a country newspaper, as well as earning an actual living with more conventional jobs.

She's looking forward to becoming a grandmother when her busy daughter can find the time, but until then writing a series of cheerful whodunits about a Scottish retirement village is definitely her favourite occupation.

Glossary

Bampot—lunatic

Blether—to have a talk, chatter, gossip.

Dinna fash—don't worry (also dinnae fash – both in common usage)

Dinnae, cannae, etc are pronounced dinny, canny

Eejit—idiot (also Irish)

Elevenses—sociable late morning tea or coffee break

Girn—complain

Hen—used to women of all ages.

HOLMES—Home Office Large Major Enquiry System - search engine for crime records.

Jag—an injection

Ken—know, I know, do you know.

Rondavel—pronounced RonDARvill – is the South African term for a round dwelling (as bungalow is an Indian word for a single-storey house)

Taken the huff—offended.

Wan, or yin – one

Zoomer – Highly unstable individual

Made in the USA
Coppell, TX
07 November 2020

40942261R00095